The Holiday Hookup

FESTIVE FUN
NOVELLA ONE

Amanda Bentley

Copyright © 2022 by Amanda Bentley

All rights reserved.

No portion of this book may be reproduced in any form without written permission from the publisher or author, except as permitted by U.S. copyright law.

This book is a work of fiction. Names, characters, businesses, events, and incidents are either products of the author's imagination or used in a fictitious manner. Any resemblance to actual events or persons is purely coincidental.

Cover Design: A.R. Rose

ISBN (paperback): 979-8-9868923-0-6

The Holiday Hookup (Festive Fun # 1)

Amanda Bentley Books LLC

amandabentleybooks@gmail.com

Contents

Dedication	V
Playlist	VII
1. Chapter One	1
2. Chapter Two	11
3. Chapter Three	21
4. Chapter Four	31
5. Chapter Five	43
6. Chapter Six	63
7. Chapter Seven	67
8. Chapter Eight	73
9. Chapter Nine	83
10. Chapter Ten	93
Bonus Chapter	103
Also By Amanda Bentley	104
Acknowledgments	105

To readers who love a rollercoaster ride…

This is just the queue.

Playlist

Listen on Spotify!

1. "Shout Out to My Ex" by Little Mix

2. "I Knew You Were Trouble (Taylor's Version)" by Taylor Swift

3. "Perfect" by One Direction

4. "Let's Fall in Love for the Night" by FINNEAS

5. "Santa Tell Me" by Ariana Grande

6. "bad ones" by Tate McRae

7. "Somebody I F*cked Once" by Zolita

8. "Hooked" by Why Don't We

9. "bad idea!" by girl in red

10. "River" by BRKN LOVE

Chapter One

December 22nd

"Still a no show?" Dave, the bartender I just met tonight, says to me with that hideous look in his eyes. That look I know so well—*pity*.

"His loss, right?" I say flippantly, hiding the true dismay I feel while I twirl the festive red straw around in my fancy gingerbread-something drink. Maybe he couldn't leave a holiday party early, or had to attend to family. It is December 22nd, after all.

He would have rescheduled, dumbass. He just didn't show.

"Damn right. I'd never stand a pretty girl like you up," he says with a flirtatious wink. If he wasn't so... *not* what I was looking for, his compliment might have cheered me up. He's got to be in his forties, which is a bit older than my twenty-five-year-old self.

I'm all for love who you love, but I've personally never wanted a man that's older. The no-show guy I met on Tinder claimed to be twenty-eight, but that remains to be seen. Or would have been, I suppose. I should have known by his name—Brad. It just *screams* fuckboy.

Maybe I'm being presumptuous. Or post-sumptuous, as the case may be. Either way, if I have to sit here sucking down this sugary excuse for a cocktail surrounded by Christmas twinkle lights for a second longer, I might gag. I doubt Dave wants to clean *that* up.

"I'll go ahead and close out," I tell the bartender as he finishes making a pair of drinks.

"It's on the house, sweetheart. Better luck next time." He rushes to get the drinks to a couple a few seats away, who smile cheerfully at him.

Maybe I should give older guys a try. At least they compliment me and buy me a damn drink.

"Thanks," I say with a wave. Rising from the bar seat, I grab my purse from the chair back and adjust my clothing. I look damn cute tonight, too, with my tight black, high-waisted skirt that lands mid-thigh, showing off the exposed part of my long legs in black, knee-high boots.

My matching long-sleeved blouse with a white-and-black window pane pattern is tucked into the front of my skirt. The two buttons off the right collarbone help accentuate my curves and give voluptuous shape to my breasts. Paired with my hair in a tight bun and light makeup, I think I pull off classy and edgy well. I wore my square, black-rimmed glasses rather than my contacts tonight, thinking they really solidified the outfit.

Just a waste of time.

I glance around and realize in the thirty or so minutes I sat, waiting for no-show, fuckboy Brad, the place filled up. This bar opened a few months ago and it's been a hotspot ever since, but I figured places like these didn't fill up until 9 or 10 pm. I glance at my black leather wristwatch and confirm it's only 8:30 pm.

I shake my wrist, adjust the strap on my shoulder, and move towards the exit. I'm about to make it out scot-free when I'm bumped on the shoulder. Irritated, I look over and come face-to-face with the exact reason for knowing the look of pity so well: my ex-boyfriend.

He hasn't noticed me yet and I need to get the fuck out of here before he does. The last thing I need on top of being stood up is to deal with him.

But he never did make things easy for me.

"Well, well, well, look who's actually out and about," he says with a smarmy grin. It sets off the seething cauldron that's been bubbling in the recesses of my body since I realized my date was a no-show.

"Fuck off, Trent," I spit at him, turning back to the exit. But he speaks again, and I'm not sure if it's the disappointment of being stood up, the fact that I'm seeing my lying, cheating ex, or a sick mixture of both, but I'm rooted to the spot at his words.

"Oh, I did that alright." I turn my head to him slowly, unsure that I heard him right. "You made sure of that, didn't you?"

Is he seriously blaming me for his indiscretions because I preferred staying home while he wanted to go out most days of the week? His eyes hold a menacing glare, and I'm about to retaliate when none other than the *fucking* girl he cheated with and left me for sidles up next to him.

"Hey, babe—" Gillian cuts herself off when her wide eyes meet my icy stare. Yeah, I know her name. I have this unyielding need to have answers to everything in my life. So when Trent broke up with me and told me he'd been cheating—hey, at least he was honest—I staked out his house until I saw her show up. A few social media searches later, and I had a name.

I didn't do anything with the information. Just obsessed over who she was, what she studied, where she worked, and what friends she had. Anything to clue me in as to why she was better than me. Weeks turned into months, and a year later, I put Trent and his bullshit behind me.

I've dated on and off, but you know as well as I do how that's gone. I was supposed to meet *fuckboy Brad* tonight. So yeah, it's gone **great**.

But you know what? I'm not the same girl Trent left, and it's time he damn well knows it.

WHAM.

My fist lands on Trent's cheek before I can process what I've done. My knuckles ache instantly, but I shake them out with a malicious grin. Gillian's eyes bug out of her skull, and she takes a few staggered steps back. Trent holds the right side of his face and pegs me with an incredulous look.

"What the fuck, you bitch!"

It would be more classy, and certainly clever of me, to give him a sassy, one-line response, then walk the fuck out of here like I own the place.

Instead, I drop my purse and walk up to him, grab him by the shoulders, and knee him right in the dick before he can process what I'm doing.

"Ahhh!" Gillian's exaggerated shriek demands the attention of the bar, and all eyes are on us as I step back and retrieve my purse from the ground. I dust it off as I fix it back on my shoulder, placing a sweet smile on my face that opposes the hatred and shock I feel inside.

I'm about to give that one-line response when an arm wraps around my waist, pulling me into a firm, warm body. I snap my head back and find a man I've never met before, dressed in all black, planted next to me.

"There you are, baby. I was wondering where you'd run off to." He glowers at Trent, who straightens at his words.

"I—erm—uh—" The shock of this random guy coupled with my actions renders me speechless.

"I'm sure whatever Mr. Asshole did to deserve your fist—and knee—was well-earned." His voice is all silk, goosebumps erupting over my skin. He places a kiss on my head and my breath hitches when I catch a glimpse of his face. "Saves me the trouble of having to scuff him up myself."

The physical attack on Trent was about all I'm capable of in terms of spontaneous action. The adrenaline coursing through my veins is begging for more, but my brain is trying to catch up to what's going on. Luckily, this guy seems to pick up on that fact, rushing us towards the exit before Trent, Gillian, or anyone else can speak.

The cold wind whips the exposed skin of my legs as we walk out, but the slight warmth from his tight grip on my hip is all I can focus on. The temperature in our town, Azalea Pines, never drops below forty. I didn't bother bringing a jacket, thinking I wouldn't spend much time outside, but I'm now chastising myself for not planning properly.

The moment we're down the street, I peel myself off of mystery man and gawk at him. "Who the hell are you?!" The absence of his hand on my hip is strangely pronounced, and I find myself wishing it was still there. It must be an effect of the adrenaline. Or the cold.

"A thanks would suffice," he replies with a smirk. It's not like the one Trent wore, though. His is teasing and confident in a pleasant way, not in an 'I'm better than you' way. Now that we're away from that whole... whatever the fuck that run-in was, because I *refuse* to process that now, I take in his appearance.

I knew he was taller than me, and sturdy, but now I find that he's attractive, too. Okay, not just attractive, straight-up edible. It's as if he was drawn up by my own imagination, hitting every check mark on what I find hot as hell on a guy. Well, except for the eyebrow piercing. But it's totally working for him.

Stop checking him out.

His twinkling eyes force me back to earth. My frustration builds again, because here I am with this sexy guy who just pulled me away from assaulting my ex. My cheeks redden with mortification, sending me on the defense.

"I was handling things fine on my own, I didn't need—"

"Oh, I know. It was awesome." I blink and he continues. "I wanted to throw more gas on the fire. I thought it could be fun." He shrugs, as if that's really all it was. And I should have no reason *not* to believe him.

But my trust in men is shit. Cases in point—asshole, cheating Trent and no-show, fuckboy Brad.

"Well—" Unable to finish that sentence with anything coherent, I settle on learning who he is. "Who are you?"

"Lorenzo."

"Kate," I respond automatically, as if he cares who I am.

"For Katherine or Caitlin?"

"Just Kate." No one calls me by my full name, Katherine, and I'd like to keep it that way.

"Well, it's a pleasure." That grin hasn't left his face, his eyebrows arched in amusement.

"I'm not going to say thank you because I didn't *ask* for your help."

"Come on. You gotta admit, that was the cherry on top of a badass sundae."

As much as I hate to admit it, he's not wrong. I'd be lying if I said I didn't feel... exhilarated from what just happened.

"I just... I haven't been able to process any of this."

"What is there to process? You hit some douchebag right in his shit and crotch-splotched him for—what?"

I'm cackling, unable to control myself. I'm not sure what's come over me. Maybe that gingerbread drink had something other than alcohol in it.

"I'm—sorry," I choke out between laughs. "Crotch-splotched?"

I wipe the tears that have formed in my crinkled eyes and he frowns. "That's an expression, isn't it?"

The giggles settle and I gather myself. "I've never heard it before, but it's highly appropriate."

"Well, you crotch-splotched him"—his use of the phrase sends me into a fit of giggles again, which he ignores—"for good measure, and I'm sure he and his girlfriend will never forget it."

The mention of Gillian subdues me instantly. Lorenzo must sense it, because he gives me *that* look.

"Don't." I shake my head, begging myself to regain composure. "I'm not some badass. I never do anything like this, ever. I... don't know what came over me."

It felt freaking amazing, though.

"That doesn't make it any less badass. Obviously, it's in you."

I don't know how to tell him how wrong he is, so I stay quiet for a moment. He doesn't fill the silence either, only watching me with curious eyes.

"I, well, thanks, I guess," I finally mutter.

"You didn't ask for it, so no thanks are necessary." The lack of bitterness in his tone makes it seem like he genuinely means it.

I give him a half-hearted smile. "I'm gonna go."

"Where's your car?"

"Oh, I didn't drive. I Ubered." I don't need to tell him that I *don't* drive. When my parents were teaching me to drive, I backed up into Dad's parked car in the driveway. I had a panic attack and refused to ever drive again. At this point, I wish I would just grow the courage to learn, but over the years the fear has become anxiety inducing. Plus, our town is like a city in a lot of ways. I don't need a car.

Lorenzo nods. "Well, I can at least wait until your driver gets here. What if that guy—"

"Trent." The name leaves a trail of acid on my tongue, and it's evident in my tone. Why I felt the need for Lorenzo to know his name is besides me. Blame it on my Type A personality, I guess.

"What if *Trent* decides to come outside and sees you alone? The cat will be out of the bag."

"That's true," I say with a thoughtful nod. I did the damn thing, after all, so may as well see it through properly. "Although, he could see you walk back in without me."

"It makes sense that I waited for you to leave before returning inside. If I go in without you, and then you're standing outside alone, it would make no sense."

"I guess." I pull out my phone and open the Uber app, requesting a ride. "Okay, the driver is three minutes away."

"Cool." He keeps his eyes on me, apparently not afraid of that new person interaction. He must be one of those extroverted types. My nose wrinkles of its own accord.

"What?" Lorenzo asks.

"Nothing, you're just…"

"Charming? Good-natured? Intelligent?"

I snort. "Not all at once, please."

He shrugs with a lopsided grin, a dimple forming below his cheek. "Nothing wrong with knowing your value, Kate."

"Knowing it and showing it off are two *totally* separate things."

"Are you calling me a show-off?" He feigns offense by raising his hand to his chest, but I see that stupid twinkle in his eyes and I'm not fooled.

I roll my eyes and glance down at my phone. One minute.

"I left my jacket inside, do you want me to grab it?" He must be responding to my chattering teeth.

"No, the driver's one minute away."

He nods once.

"Did you drive here?" I ask because unlike him, I'm not comfortable in awkward silences.

"Oh, I'm not leaving. I only arrived a few minutes before you crotch-splotched that dude." That gets a laugh out of me. Seeming pleased, Lorenzo continues. "I'll go back to my friends once you're gone."

Once I'm gone. Because no one *really* wants to spend time with me. Lorenzo said it himself—it seemed like fun. That's all this was.

As if on cue, tires screech next to the sidewalk where we stand, and I slip my phone into my purse.

"Thanks for waiting with me."

"And for acting like your boyfriend back there."

I roll my eyes. "Both highly unnecessary." I open the backseat door of the car, waving at the driver.

"Both *fun.*"

Our gazes lock for a moment, my stomach swirling with stupid butterflies. I get into the car, but as I'm shutting the door, he grabs the frame and says, "Merry Christmas."

"Happy Holidays." I squeeze my lips into a tight-lipped smile and finish shutting the door, letting the driver take me away. I glance through the back windshield when we're about to turn the corner, finding Lorenzo watching the car with his hands in his pockets.

I'm officially done with relationships, I decide. Trent cheated and left me for someone else, which according to him was my fault. Brad literally didn't see any potential in me, seeing as he stood me up without a word. I don't need to check the app to know he's probably blocked me. Not that I'd reach out— that's all sorts of desperate.

Lorenzo was really cute.

Cute is an understatement, but we're not going there. I refuse to think anymore about him. He didn't even ask for my number— that's telling enough. It's the nail in the coffin of my love life, because even my just-met, fake boyfriend didn't *actually* want me.

Chapter Two

December 23rd

"Champagne, ma'am?"

I'm startled when the server carrying a tray full of sparkly, disposable flutes meets me at the entry of the mini-mansion.

"Um, sure." I take one from his tray and he scurries back to the corner, ready to pounce on the next guest that walks in.

My boss, co-owner of the company, throws a holiday party every year for our branch. He calls it a holiday party, but it's very obviously a Christmas party. Not that it bothers me, but if you're going to call it a holiday party, it should include all of the holidays, right?

I face the vast living room, finding the place decked out in Christmas—not holiday—decorations from floor to ceiling. Lights are strung across the second story railings that wrap around the three walls in front of me.

I take the single step down from the entryway into the living room and glance around, confirming I'm the first to arrive. I've never understood why people always arrive late to a party. What's the point of putting a time if you're not going to adhere to it? Why not just list 'evening' or 'afternoon'?

"Kate! Punctual as always," Rowan Valeri says.

"Someone's gotta be first," I tell him with a grin. He's a great boss—it's why I accepted his job offer after interning at his brokerage for a year. I started my internship the week before the holiday break four years ago, and I've been an underwriter ever since. Despite my proffer to start upon the return to the office, Rowan insisted that I attend the holiday party. "It's a great way to get acquainted with your new coworkers," he'd said.

"Well I'm happy to know that someone is still you. Make yourself at home. Lily will be out in a few minutes and others should trickle in soon."

He rushes out to the patio through the open french doors. The entire back wall of his house is floor-to-ceiling windows, overlooking the luscious pool deck and lawn. I peruse the spread of appetizers on the table and shoo off the two different servers who ask if I need anything.

With my champagne and small plate of bread and cheese, I travel out to the patio deck and take a seat at one of the many tables set up with decorative red and white table cloths. I pull my phone out of my purse and check my text messages.

Char: still no word from Brad?

Oh, Charlotte. The eternal optimist. When I talked to her this morning, she insisted that Brad must have fallen ill or had some other sort of emergency that caused him not to show. I couldn't stop myself from double—*fine,* triple—checking the app to make sure he didn't message me. Just as I knew, he hadn't, which meant he just didn't want to meet me.

After I'd checked Tinder, I mulled over the run-in with Trent. Or rather, I mulled over his words. *You made sure of that, didn't you?* Bile rises in my throat. We were together for nearly two years. While he did confess to cheating while he was breaking up with me, it still broke my heart. It still shattered my trust with men.

That's why it's better if I don't date. I told Char as much, to which she rolled her eyes and demanded I stop being dramatic. It's easy for her to say. She has a hot date every other week, choosing not to settle down because she simply hasn't found *the one*.

I scoff, tearing off a piece of bread and stuffing it in my mouth with a cube of cheese. I type out my reply as I chew.

Me: Let it go. I'm not messaging him.

Char: I'm not letting it go

Char: you need to get laid

No arguments there, Char. It's the whole reason I agreed to download the freaking Tinder app to begin with. But it's been two months, and all I've had are two no-shows. If that's not a sign from the universe, I don't know what is.

To be fair, it's not like I tried that hard. Between work, my pilates sessions, and my furry cat Felix, I keep busy. I'm also not a socially driven person. As Trent pointed out, I don't want to go out all the time. I like hanging out at home with my own thoughts. Char and I have a standing Sunday brunch date, and we often see each other throughout the week. She is my best friend, after all, and living a few blocks away certainly helps.

"Hey, Kate."

My coworker, Victor, takes a seat next to me with a plate of his own food, followed closely by his boyfriend. We take up amicable conversation and twenty minutes later, the place is full of noise and bustle made by the fifty or so employees from our branch at Valeri Financials. I excuse myself from the table to start making rounds, saying hello to the others, most of which I only recognize from seeing in the halls.

If all goes well, I'll be out of here in an hour and back to cuddling Felix while watching reruns of Friends. I pause to talk with coworkers I know and their plus ones. I chat with Lily for a few minutes and when she finally excuses herself, I let out a breath. Glancing at my watch, I confirm it's 9:30 pm.

Right on schedule.

I'm about to step up on the entryway when Rowan's rushed words force me to stop.

"Kate! Come meet the new hire!"

So close.

I pivot, coming face to face with—

"Lorenzo?!" My mouth is hanging open like an ogling baboon, so I close it and blink.

"You two know each other?" Rowan says, watching us like a tennis match. He's still wearing the shit eating grin I normally appreciate.

"We met last night, actually," Lorenzo replies, his eyes glued to me. He wears the same smirk I couldn't stop thinking about as I fell asleep. It sends an unexpected wave of tingles through me. He's still in all black, but this time it's slacks and a dress shirt rather than the jeans and long-sleeved tee. "What are—"

"I ran into him at the grocery store!" I sputter out. I tear my eyes from Lorenzo and smile at Rowan, who's eyebrows crease in. *The grocery store??*

"That's right. She accidentally bumped my car with her cart. Thought I was gonna have to put in an insurance claim." His smirk widens and that stupid twinkle appears in his eyes.

Luckily, Rowan laughs. *I* do not. Rowan says something I don't process, then walks off, leaving me standing here with Lorenzo.

I round on him immediately. "Seriously? Bumped your car? You couldn't come up with anything else?"

"It was that or watch your eyes bug out of your skull. Don't get your panties in a bunch, princess."

There must be fumes emitting from the top of my head. A server walks by with a tray of champagne flutes, and I grab two before he even notices. Lorenzo reaches out a hand but I throw one of the flutes completely back, followed by the second.

Because this is a joke, right? Some sick, twisted joke that the universe is playing on me. How in the world is Lorenzo starting at our firm? I went to bed last night storing the box that contained the memory of running into Trent on the 'did not happen' shelf.

Holding the empty flutes, I grit my teeth. "Can I speak with you outside for a moment?"

I stalk off to a removed area of the yard, dumping the plastic flutes in the trash bin I pass. The nearby bushes provide a glow from the lights strung along every inch of them. I spin around, facing—no one.

What the hell? Where did he go? I glance around, locating him talking to some employees at the closest table. I roll my eyes and sigh, my mind reeling at the speed of light.

I need to get this under control, STAT. I didn't even tell Char about last night's aggression, because that would require acknowledging it really happened.

Lorenzo finally walks over, at a very unhurried pace I might add.

"I meant immediately," I snap when he finally plants himself in front of me, crossing his arms over his chest. I can't help but notice the way his muscles pull on his arm sleeves.

He makes a quick sweep of me, his eyes narrowing. "What happened to your glasses?"

As much as it flatters me that he remembered what I wore, I decide to cut straight to the point. "Look. I told you last night, that person is not who I am. I don't know what got into me. But that debacle—"

"The crotch-splotch."

My lips twitch but I refuse to laugh. "That stays between us."

He doesn't reply, only fixing his stance as he stares at me. I hold his eye, ignoring the desire to see them twinkle again.

"You're kind of a brat," he finally says.

"Excuse me?" My hands form fists at my side.

"What, no one's ever told you that before?"

Angry tears burn at the back of my eyes from the sheer *audacity* of this fucking guy. Thank god he didn't ask for my number last night, because I probably would have given it to him.

"Don't worry, I like it," he says when he realizes his effect on me.

"I'm not worried about what you do or don't like, Lorenzo," I spit at him.

This must be a dream. I'm snuggled up in my bed, Felix at my head, and I'll wake at any moment. I drink in his features one last time, committing them to memory for future use with my vibrator. Because no matter how frustrating he's being right now, I can't deny my utter attraction to him.

"Hey, I didn't mean to offend you." I tear my gaze from his eyebrow stud and take in his frown. Obviously, this is not a dream, and I can't just stand here without responding.

"I'm not sure how else you'd expect someone *you don't even know* to respond after being called a brat."

"Aw, come on. I know you pretty well. Just last night, you were my girlfriend."

"Shh!" I glance around to make sure no one heard his words.

"Tell me something, Kate." I meet his amused yet contemplative stare. "Why are you so ashamed of your badassery?"

"I'm not ashamed!" *Okay, maybe just a little.* "This is my boss's house—"

"Our boss's house."

"—and I can't very well be known for punching my ex—"

"And crotch-splotching him."

"—It's unprofessional and—"

"Badass."

"Would you stop?" I roar. That gets a few heads turning our way, but I refuse to make eye contact with anyone but the man in front of me. I continue in a heated whisper. "Look what you're making me do! I don't know what fucked up universe I'm living in, but just because you saw me out of sorts yesterday does not give you the right to disrupt my life!"

I cross my arms over my chest and huff, holding back the foot stomp because I can't give more ammunition to this brat thing. Lorenzo's smirk dissolves into a studious look, his eyes volleying between mine.

"I'd never mention that around our coworkers. Or boss, for that matter. For the record, I was going to tell Rowan we met through mutual friends, but apparently you had no trust in me. So I thought it would be fun to play with you a bit. Because come on, grocery store? Really?"

Friends would have been a much better excuse. Not that I'll ever admit that to him.

"I don't know you. Why in the world would I trust you?"

I've apparently found his weakness, because he doesn't have a quick remark to that. But it's true, isn't it?

"You have my word. I won't tell a soul about last night," he finally says.

"Thank you."

"Except for my roommate."

"Lorenzo!"

"What? He saw what happened."

Ugh. Why didn't I just walk away last night?

Do you really wish you had, though?

"And just so you know, as I was walking back into the bar, your ex was leaving with that girl and a group of friends. He was still holding his hand to his cheek, so you should be proud."

Against my self-control, I do smile at that. Fuck Trent.

"See? Being a badass is great. Revel in it, Kate."

I shake my head. "It's not who I am."

"I'd beg to differ."

I glance around again, thankful no one is paying us any attention. I'm not going to argue with Lorenzo about who I am or not. I know me, he doesn't.

"Well, welcome to the team. Rowan is great. Guess I'll see you Monday, then."

"You mean Wednesday?"

Christmas is Monday, doofus.

I grit my teeth. "Right."

"What, so you're leaving? The party just started." He takes a step closer, crowding my space.

"I don't—"

"Stay."

Chapter Three

December 23rd

He takes another step, slipping his hand around my waist and pulling me into him. I'm frozen at the thrill it sends through me. I should be aghast. I should push him away. I should tell him to stop. But his hand sliding under my dress, gliding over my cheek, feels too damn good. The idea that anyone could—

That does the trick. I shove his shoulders, his fingertips brushing my ass and swinging to his side. He still has that smirk on his face, apparently unabashed by his actions.

"Are you crazy? We're at *Rowan's. House*. Surrounded by coworkers!"

"I haven't forgotten, princess. But that dress you're wearing does make me a little crazy, I'll admit."

I glance down on reflex, as if I needed to remember what I'm wearing. I chose this outfit as meticulously as I choose all of my outfits. It's a red, long-sleeved, a-line skater dress. The sleeves are made of lace and the end has a white trim. My sparkly, silver heels match the silver necklace that hangs perfectly between my breasts, and my hair is styled in its usual bun, this time with a curl on each side of my face.

Classy and elegant.

"Did I not make myself clear a moment ago? That's not who I am. I'm not this badass, daring woman you seem to think I am."

"See, that's where I think you're wrong. I may have only met you at the grocery store last night"—his smirk grows and the twinkle returns to his eyes—"but I know a badass when I meet one."

The raw attraction I feel for him is the only reason I haven't stormed out of here. I want to—no, need to—tear my eyes away from his, but I can't. That twinkle is holding me captive, and I want to feel his hand on my ass again. Both hands, actually. I want to kiss his perfect lips—

"I'll take your silence as affirmation." He takes a step towards me, unfreezing me.

"No! I... I'm confused. If you were interested in me, why didn't you ask for my number?"

He shrugs. "Did you want me to ask for your number, Kate?"

"I—" *Yes.* "It doesn't matter. I'm not looking for a boyfriend."

"I don't want to be your boyfriend."

That's not the response I expected. "Then... what?"

"We can just fool around. Have *fun*. Come on, you can't tell me you didn't feel a rush after last night."

He took a few steps while he spoke and he's stealing all my air again, suffocating me. His words unsettle me because they're true—I did feel a rush.

And it felt fucking *good*.

I peer at him through my lashes. His eyes look like fire and smoke as they rake my body. A tremor shoots up my spine and down my arms. But then I remember where we are. I take a step back, glancing around and shaking my head.

"This isn't the time or place. Isn't this your first time meeting everyone? What is wrong with you?"

"People hook up at parties all the time. Something tells me Rowan wouldn't care what I do with his... employees," Lorenzo says, his voice full of heat and promise of what he could do to me. My pussy aches and my clit throbs desperately.

I need to stop this. Taking a step to the side, I say, "I'm gonna go. You should get to know everyone and I'll... see you Wednesday."

His smirk falters but he recuperates it in the next breath. "You don't want to get to know me, Kate?"

I don't know how to answer that. Because I do, but I don't want him to know that. I hardly want to admit it to myself. I want to know what's under all that dark apparel...

"Stay and have a few drinks. I'm sure you didn't drive, and—"

"What makes you so sure of that?" I don't like the way he presumes to know me, even if he is correct.

"You seem like the cautious type."

Okay, well he's not wrong there. And whatever... *this* is, it's the furthest thing from it. Engaging in this would be throwing caution to the wind, giving in to chasing that feeling I unlocked when I punched Trent. And crotch-splotched him.

"What are you thinking?" Lorenzo says with an arched brow, responding to the smile playing at my lips.

I wipe the smile from my face and ignore his question. "Fine. I'll stay. But only for an hour."

He only gives me an answering smirk before pivoting and strolling back towards the party. I follow him, stopping when he returns to the table he was at. More employees have joined, so he introduces himself and plugs right into the conversations.

How is he more popular than I am, and I've worked here for years? I don't even remember these people's names. We're in different departments, so I only recognize them by face. Maybe he knew someone who works with us, and that's how he got a job with Rowan.

I should be paying attention to the conversation so I can do anything other than stand by his side. Won't people wonder the same thing I'm wondering? Why am I standing with the new guy? But my mind is reeling from the choice to stay and the desire to learn everything I can about him.

We're at our third table stop, where he chats animatedly with some of the employees from IT, when I decide I'm just going to leave. Other than normal greetings, I've said nothing. I'm following him around like some sad puppy dog, and for what?

Why didn't I just go home? Why? For some reason, I followed. For some reason, I stayed. Maybe it was the two flutes of champagne I chugged, which have made their effects known.

I'll admit it's been nice just watching him… be. He's charming and personable, and people are drawn to him like a magnet. I watch his lips move as they speak, wondering what they'd feel like moving against mine. His laugh sends tingles up my spine, and I envision what it would be like to share a cup of coffee at a café.

But then I remember that I swore off men, and the heat in my core sizzles out.

Standing to his left, I wait until he's talking again and then make my move to leave. I take one step when his hand whips out and grabs my wrist, pulling me back to him. He drops it immediately and without breaking from his conversation.

What if someone saw that? What do all these people, who I—*we*—work with, think of me just standing beside him like we're best fucking pals or something?

I glance at the employees at the table, and only one girl seems to have noticed, her eyes moving from where he held my wrist to my face, then back to Lorenzo's. I think her name is Sara, but I can't be sure.

I don't have to stay anywhere I don't want to. I'm about to leave—again—when he tells the group he's going to get a drink. He nods toward me, his pierced brow arching, and I hate that it brings the heat back to my core.

I follow him into the house. When we get to the bar, he orders two shots of Fireball.

"Make it one," I tell the bartender, then turn to Lorenzo. "I'm gonna go."

"I want two," he tells the bartender. In a lower voice, he says to me, "Why?"

"I'm tired and I'm done. I was supposed to leave"—I check my watch—"an hour ago. Felix and Friends are waiting."

He looks as though I've slapped him. "You have a boyfriend?"

The confusion only lasts me a moment. "Oh, Felix is my cat."

His expression returns to its previous amused one that I'm learning is his norm. "And why are your friends at your apartment?"

I laugh at that. "No, Friends like the show."

"Oh. I don't watch much TV."

The bartender slides the shot glasses over and Lorenzo takes them. He nods his head towards the entryway and the ship my heart sails on feels like it was punctured because he's accepting me leaving.

Stupid heart, you don't know what you want.

When we get on the landing, he holds out a shot. "Drink with me."

"Why do you keep insisting on hanging out with me?"

He eyes me for a moment before responding. "I like you."

My head jerks back in disbelief. "You just corralled me around while you talked to a bunch of people. Then, I decline the shot and you order me one anyway. What are you playing at?"

He frowns. "I'm new. I've got to make good first impressions."

I guess that's true. "I thought you didn't want to be my boyfriend?" I can't help the bitterness that seeps into my tone.

"I don't. I thought *you* said you don't want a boyfriend," he fires back.

"I don't."

"So what's the problem?"

"What is this?"

He has the nerve to look annoyed. "*Fun.* You said a few drinks, and you haven't even agreed to this first one."

I eye the shot glass he holds out, and he huffs. "Get out of your head and into the moment."

Fuck him. He doesn't know me.

I take the glass from him and he smirks, then holds his up. "To being coworkers." As I raise my glass, he adds, "And badassery."

I roll my eyes and clink his glass, shooting back the shot. The cinnamon whiskey burns down my throat and leaves a pleasant tingle on my tongue. I raise my head and lick my bottom lip, finding Lorenzo's eyes pinned to my mouth, full of heat.

My pussy throbs without my consent, pining for that look and what it leads to.

"Time for another," he says, his eyes boring into mine. Can he see what he's doing to me? The instant effect he has over me?

I break eye contact and turn back to the bar. I order two shots and the bartender rushes to pour them as Lorenzo steps up next to me, placing his elbows on the small counter.

"Introduce me to your coworkers," he says. I look outside, seeing Victor surrounded by our department at the table I left him at earlier. I turn back when I hear the bartender place our drinks on the counter.

Lorenzo reaches for one of the glasses, bringing it just under his nose. "Jägermeister, interesting choice."

"Nothing interesting about it, Lorenzo. It's a great drink."

"It is." His tongue flicks across his lips before he takes the shot, making it my turn to stare. He places the empty glass atop the counter, the bartender clearing it immediately. "I'll take another Fireball, on the rocks this time. And for you? A vodka-cran?"

I don't think it was his intention, but the fact that he thinks he's got me pegged as some basic girl who likes basic drinks really ticks me off. Vodka-cran is a *great* drink, by the way. It's a solid choice and always satisfies.

"I'll have what you're having," I say instead of agreeing to my go-to cocktail, because fuck him. The bartender gets to work and I take my shot of Jäger while we wait.

"Remember, not a word about last night. And keep your paws to yourself, I don't need rumors flying around when they couldn't be further from the truth," I warn Lorenzo.

"Chill, princess. I'm not a wild animal."

I grit my teeth. "And don't call me princess."

"Fine," he says, a pleasant smile stretched on his face. When the bartender places our drinks on the counter, I lead us to the table and approach my coworkers.

"Hey, guys," I say with a bright, cheery smile plastered on my face. "This is one of the new hires, Lorenzo." When Victor gives me a curious look, I add, "Rowan wanted me to show him around."

Lorenzo's eyebrow twitches. So what if it was a lie? I can't explain the *real* reason I'm introducing him.

Because he's hot as all hell and you can't help but be near him.

"Welcome to the family," Victor says, holding his hand out for Lorenzo. "This is my boyfriend, Joey." They shake and Lorenzo takes one of the empty seats. I hesitate a moment before taking the one next to him.

"This is Alexandra, Matteo, Jeremy, Dominique, and Jasmine," I say, pointing to each person as I introduce them. They smile or wave while Lorenzo nods to each of them. "We make up the finance department."

"So you're the ones making sure I get paid. Excellent," Lorenzo says while looking at me, then turns his attention to the group. I don't miss the twinkle that was in his eyes as everyone laughed.

Just as before, he makes instant chatter with everyone, leaving me wondering if he's the new hire or I am. Jasmine, who's seated next to me, asks me a question about the upcoming audit, and I'm swept into a conversation with her.

The tablecloth tickles my thigh, and I glance down but don't notice anything. Returning my attention to Jasmine, I listen to her plan for the next month when I feel a rough, warm hand on my thigh. I jump in surprise, my knee banging into one of the table's bars.

"Are you okay?" Jasmine asks, glancing down. I follow her line of sight but there's nothing to see.

"Yeah, I, uh, think there was a bug or something," I say. But the hand on my thigh squeezes, then starts to rub its palm against my thigh. I squirm a bit and my cheeks instantly burn. While Jasmine keeps rambling about the next month's tight schedule, I glance over to Lorenzo's lap.

Sure enough, his arm cuts off at the bicep, hidden beneath the tablecloth. I look up at him but he's listening intently to Victor. His lip tilts up, though.

Sneaky son of a bitch.

I'm deathly afraid someone will notice what he's doing, but god it feels so fucking good. I don't want him to stop, which equally scares and excites me. When his fingers reach my inner thigh, he gives a light squeeze before rubbing his palm back to my outer thigh.

Over and over, his hand tortures me and my panties dampen from the tease. My clit pulses, wanting more. Needing more. If he would just move his hand higher, right to my—

You're at your work holiday party!

That snaps me out of my hypnosis, and I choke down a sip of Fireball.

"Lorenzo! What department will you be working in?" He turns to me, his expression neutral and impassive, as if he's not working his hand slowly up my thigh and towards my burning, soaking center.

"Marketing. Web design, specifically," he replies effortlessly. His lips are curved up ever so slightly, and I can't be sure I'm not imagining it simply because I know what he's doing to me.

"Oh, thank god. Our website needs work," Matteo says. I tear my eyes from Lorenzo and realize that everyone listened to my question.

Damn it. This distraction plan backfired.

As Lorenzo starts answering questions about his studies, I slip my hand under the table and grab his hand, intending to move it off my leg. But he grabs my fingers, stroking the back with his thumb before clasping my hand in his.

His hand is significantly larger than mine. I could fight to release my hand, but too much movement would give us away. He moves my hand over my pussy and cups it, his fingers brushing across my entrance.

How is he able to focus on what anyone is saying? I sure as fuck can't. His middle finger strokes the wetness on my panties, and it takes everything in me not to moan.

I shouldn't want to moan. I shouldn't be enjoying this. Trent was the last person I had sex with, and I can't remember ever feeling this enthralled. I'm on great terms with my vibrator, but that only takes you so far. I barely even know Lorenzo, and he's making me feel better than I have in a long time.

But we're at our *work* holiday party, and this isn't who I am.

I shoot up so suddenly that I hear the drop of his hand on the leg of his chair. Everyone's eyes shoot to me and he quickly moves his hand to his lap, so I don't think anyone noticed.

"I need to use the bathroom." I set my drink on the table and turn, not missing the look in Lorenzo's eyes when I do my best to calmly walk to the bathroom.

Locking myself into the safety of the square room, I remove my panties and sit on the toilet. I've never been more thankful that I wore my red lace bra and panty set instead of the boyshorts I usually like. Not like he's even seen them. But guys can tell from touch alone, right?

I bet Lorenzo can. The way he was grabbing me and tantalizing me, he probably does this all the time. Maybe he was fired from his previous job for getting frisky with the staff. He flat out said he doesn't want to be my boyfriend. Which is perfect, because I'm done with men.

Right?

I've never been the one-night stand type. I'm a homebody, and that requires a whole lot of effort that I don't put into going out and meeting people. I'm not opposed to the idea, but this just seems downright foolish.

We're coworkers now. This can't end well, one way or the other. The distance I forced on us is clearing my head.

It's time to go home.

Chapter Four

December 23rd

I finish peeing and wipe not only myself but my panties, still slick with my desire. The desire I'm stifling. As I wash my hands, my head spins and it dawns on me that the shots we took are in effect. I wish I could message Char about this, but she doesn't know about Lorenzo, and it's too much to explain through a measly text.

I'll call her as soon as I get home.

My naked eyes stare back at me as I dry my hands with a paper towel. Tonight I went with contacts because this outfit didn't fit the glasses vibe. I tighten my lips and exit the bathroom, walking down the empty hallway towards the party. Suddenly, I'm shoved into the wall.

"Not so fast." His voice is right in my ear, his chest crowding me in and his hips digging into my back. I feel my body weaken in response, leaning into the touch I so desperately crave. My ass rubs on his slacks and I want nothing more than to grind against him, to feel his cock harden on it.

But I find the willpower to whip around and shove him back. "Are you crazy?" I hiss. "Anyone can see us!" I look behind him, but everyone is distracted, absorbed in the party.

"We're in the dark here, princess." His tone matches his smoldering eyes, roaming over me like I'm his first meal after being starved for a week. "Or am I still not allowed to call you that?"

"I need to understand what is happening!" I shout-whisper. I try to leave but he boxes me in with his palms pressed into the walls on either side.

"What's there to understand? I want you and you want me. Don't try to deny it, Kate. I *felt* it. I still feel it."

It's a good thing we are in this dark hallway, because my cheeks just turned ten shades darker.

"You want me to stop? Say it." Seconds tick by, but I can't get myself to utter the words my brain is shouting at me to say. His body feels too good against mine. The heat emanating from his chest is melting my insides, and I want his hand back on my thigh. And on my hips. I want them *everywhere*.

"You want me. And I..." He leans in, sending a shiver up my spine when his forearms brush my shoulders. "I want to *ruin* you."

I let out a low moan before I can stop it, my back arching so my chest touches his. His hands travel to my waist, squeezing and rubbing in a perfect rhythm. I start to grind against him, forgetting myself. Someone laughs, the travel echoing down the hallway, and I freeze.

"We can't stay here!"

"Fine. Come on." *Finally, some sense!* He grabs my hand and tows me into the living room, where the majority of our coworkers are mingling. The energy here has shifted since people first arrived. It's more lively, more intoxicating. The Christmas tree in the corner mocks me, reminding me exactly where we are.

I pull my hand out of his, refusing to let anyone see what's going on. He winks at me but doesn't try to take it back, simply walking towards the front door. Will we go to his place or mine? Do I even want him at my place? I'm pretty sure I left my dishes from earlier in the sink. I can't let him see that!

We reach the entryway but he surprises me by turning left towards the stairs behind the wall that separates the living room. When he takes a step up, I start laughing. He turns and faces me with his lips curled into a predatory smile. There's humor in it... but something much darker, too.

"You can't be serious," I whisper, looking around to make sure we're alone. His smile only deepens, his eyes clouded by lust, and I realize he's one hundred percent serious. I also realize he's bat shit crazy.

"Be that badass for one more night, Kate. No one ever has to know and—"

I burst into laughter. He's out of his fucking mind. "No one has to know? You understand you're walking up the stairs of *Rowan's* house. Our boss!" It hits me again, the insanity of all of this. That this random man standing in front of me pretended to be my boyfriend after I assaulted my ex-boyfriend. And now, he's going to be working with me. He already *is* working with me.

This is downright reckless.

"You know how to be quiet, don't you?" His eyes study mine and when I don't respond, he adds, "I bet you get *real* wild when you're fucking. I bet—"

"This is inappropriate! And rude. And just so.... Ah!" The frustration I'm feeling boils over. Because I want him and I shouldn't. If he really wants to do this, why doesn't he take me on a date? Get to know me?

That's right. He doesn't want to be my boyfriend. Which is fine, right? I've sworn off men. I don't want to be with him, either.

He moves off the step, standing directly in front of me. I crane my neck up and stare into his eyes. They're still dark and full of all the wicked things he's offering, but there's something else, too.

"I tell it like it is, princess. You don't want this? Walk out that door right now. I won't stop you. I won't take anything from you you're not willing to give. But don't keep telling me that this isn't who you are, or that you're not feeling exactly what I'm feeling."

"And what is that, exactly?"

"You know." His fingers stroke down my arm with a featherlight touch, and I lean into it without reservation.

I should just go. I should do exactly as he said and walk out that door, order my Uber home, and forget this ever happened. We'll run into each other in the office from time to time, and this will all be a strange, hazy memory that we can pretend never existed.

"I *saw* you last night, Kate. I saw the smoke rising in your eyes from the ashes. *You* were the fire. Keep telling yourself that's not who you are. But all you're doing is dousing the flames within you."

Fire? Flames? What in the world is he talking about? I'm a calm, collected person. Punching and hitting my ex in his junk was a... fluke. Right? It doesn't matter that I felt a rush, that it did make me feel more alive than I have in a long time. Possibly ever.

"Come on, I'll walk you out and wait for your ride." He takes a step towards the front door and I throw my hand out, curling my fingers around his upper arm. I can't help but admire the power emitting from his muscles. I squeeze and he flexes, responding to me as though by instinct.

What are you doing?

"You have to promise me that you won't tell a *soul* about this. Not even your roommate." My voice is still a whisper. He slowly faces me, his eyes seeking mine out. One side of his lips tilt up in that smirk. I'm finding myself drawn to him like a moth to a flame.

Or maybe I'm the flame, like he said.

"Your secrets are safe with me, Kate. Always."

I only nod my head, my heart racing with the realization of what I've agreed to. We're about to have sex. In our boss's house.

I'm shocked by the thrill it sends rippling through me. But the logical, *louder,* part of my brain screams at me that this is stupid.

"Why don't we go to one of our places?" I say. I glance back towards the party but no one's attention is on this tucked away, poorly lit area. I look up the stairs; it's even darker up there and completely silent.

My eyes return to Lorenzo's. He's completely focused on me, amusement etched into his features. My breath hitches when I realize he also looks fiercely determined.

"As much as I would enjoy meeting Felix, I may have lied earlier. Maybe I am a wild animal." He winks before pivoting and tiptoeing up the steps. I look around one more time before throwing caution to the wind in complete reckless abandon and follow him.

Turn around now! Go home. Don't do this. You could be caught. You could be fired!

My brain screams, shouts, and pleads with me, but for a reason I can't—or won't—identify, I ignore it. I follow Lorenzo as he turns left down the hall. There's a door at the end of it, which I have to assume is the master bedroom. Lorenzo cracks open the first door to our right. From over his shoulder, I see a navy blue painted room with a twin bed in the corner and a racecar lamp on the nightstand.

This must be Rowan and Lily's son's room.

Kate, what are you doing?!

He closes the door silently by twisting the knob and only releasing it when it's aligned with the frame. He walks to the next door down the hall and I follow closely behind. The banister overlooking the living room is right next to us, and if someone stares hard enough, they'd see us in the dark. We need to hurry.

I nudge his ribs and he opens the door, revealing a queen bed centered under a window with nightstands on either side. I squint to try and make out the painting on the wall perpendicular to the bed, but it's too dark.

"Perfect," he whispers. When his eyes land on mine, they turn to smoke, his eyelids lowering slightly. His lips land on mine so suddenly that I gasp when his tongue swipes across my upper lip. Recovering, I reach my hesitant tongue to meet his, and it feels like pure sin. He tastes so good, like cinnamon and the smoke in his eyes.

Wait—does he smoke?

I don't have time to ponder it when he distracts me by biting into my lower lip, his hands reaching my waist and ramming me up against the door frame. Everything sounds as loud as a tornado, and my eyes pop open in fear.

I find Lorenzo's eyes closed, but only for a moment. As though by instinct, they flutter open and meet mine. I feel his lips lift against mine, the smile reaching his eyes. Fuck, the way he's looking at me...

It's like I'm the only thing that matters right now. Like his hands traveling torturously slow up my front to cup my breasts, causing my nipples to harden, is all he wants to be doing. Like his mouth on mine, his tongue dancing provocatively to the same tune as my own, is the only flavor he ever wants to taste.

Maybe he was right, I do know how he feels, because it's exactly how I feel. I suck his lower lip as his tongue swipes across my upper, and we groan at the same time. Our energies are matching in perfect synchronicity. My pussy clenches with desire, sending another wave of dampness to my panties.

I tilt my hips to him but he breaks the kiss and I whimper. I *actually* whimper from the loss of the feel of his soft, pliable lips on mine. He takes one of my hands in his, giving it a light squeeze.

"I got you, don't worry. But let's get in here, just in case." His hands release my breasts and if they could cry tears, they would. He pushes the door open lightly, revealing the full room to us. There's a dresser opposite the bed and a closet opposite the painting.

This must be a guest room.

Which means Lorenzo picked up on that. And quickly. *How many times has he done this?*

I don't like the rumble that sends through my chest. Am I just going to be another notch in his metaphorical bed post? I want to ask, but it doesn't feel appropriate for... whatever this is. A one-night stand, right?

"What's going on in that badass brain of yours?"

Lorenzo's voice in my ear jolts me back to the present. He wraps his arms around my midriff and pulls me to him, reminding me why I'm here.

The bottom line is, it doesn't matter what he's done before or why he's doing this now. I made my choice. As much as I want to ask him every question I'm thinking, to know every answer so I can fully understand him, I won't.

Tonight is about fun, nothing more. Asking my questions will only put a damper on the night.

He pulls his head back after the long stretch of silence. "Kate?"

I shake my head and place my hands over his on my stomach, my palms rubbing his knuckles. That alone excites me. I might be in way over my head here. "Nothing."

The fact that he doesn't move tells me he wants to question me further, but he doesn't. A moment later, he brings his head to my neck and kisses the sensitive area near my shoulder. He would somehow know the magical key to my body.

The moan it elicits obviously pleases him, because he pushes his hips into me and inhales deeply. The rush I feel from the sound of his breath and the insanity of what we're doing is the only thing keeping me going.

Well, that and the throbbing in my clit.

My eyes dart to the door. "I locked it," he murmurs in a raspy voice. Why does it feel like he always knows what I'm thinking? Maybe he felt my head move an inch.

He grabs my hips and spins me to face him, holding me out at arms distance. His heated eyes sweep over me, lingering on my legs and chest. My stomach swoops and I find that I love the way he's looking at me.

It's like he wants to memorize this moment forever and never let it go. Or maybe that's just me.

His eyes meet mine and that swooping travels lower, right to where it aches. He licks his lips and my mouth parts.

"See, princess? You can feel how I feel, just as I feel how you feel." His fingers tighten their hold before he pulls me to him. I lean in for the kiss but he only brings his forehead to mine.

"Do you have any boundaries?"

"W–What?"

"Boundaries." He arches an eyebrow, like it's a perfectly natural question, yet I have no clue what he's talking about. "You know, like any hard passes? Things you refuse to do?"

"Oh." *Do I?* "Um, I guess if it comes up I'll let you know." I don't have any clue what he could possibly do that would require a boundary. We're just having sex, right?

He studies my face before giving a curt nod. He finally leans in to kiss me when I realize there is one and lean my head back.

"No telling *anyone* about this!" His eyes open at my words and he stares at me. "I mean it. I'm not—"

"I know, I know. This isn't who you are. Got that." He rolls his eyes and it floods my veins with ice as he moves in to kiss me again.

"If this is your idea of foreplay, it's not working." I step back and my legs hit the mattress, but I refuse to sit down. *This was a bad idea.*

"Would you stop? I don't want to do anything you're not comfortable with. And I can't help that I see a side of you that you seem stubbornly blind to."

I cross my arms over my chest with a huff. He runs his palms from my shoulders to my hands, taking them into his and pulling me close again. When our chests collide, I feel a tremor roll through my spine.

"I can't force you to feel *that*," he says. How does he know? He answers my unspoken question in a whisper, his breath hot over my face. "I feel it, too."

My heart races and I flush, rendered speechless. I do the only thing I can think to do; that feels right to do. I crash my lips onto his and moan when his tongue enters my mouth in anguished need. He groans and I feel the rumble in his chest, causing me to push my hips into him. I feel his dick harden, pressing into my stomach. I lift my hands to his shoulders, squeezing and pulling him closer.

There's one thing I can't deny— how much my body craves this. The desire to feel wanted, to orgasm, it's blocking out all the other noise. He wraps one hand around the back of my neck and the other around my waist, pulling me into his hard body so there's not an inch of space between us. Our lips clash and our hurried tongues swipe over each other.

He presses his fingers into my neck with such ferocity that it actually hurts a bit. I can feel his calluses on my skin, and it makes me want to ask him if he works out or how else he came to have them. As our mouths slow and our kiss deepens, I find myself wanting to know everything about him.

But that's not what this is, is it? This is simply for pleasure, and then we'll be on our merry ways.

He steps into me and this time, I allow my legs to bend so that I land on the mattress. He wastes no time in bringing his knee between my thighs and pushing into my center, my pussy and clit aching with his touch.

"Lorenzo," I breathe, and he smirks against my lips as he nudges his knee a few times, silently asking me to scoot back. I oblige and he brings his other knee to the bed, spreading my legs in a swift motion.

His hands on either side of my ribs cage me in. I loop my hands around his neck for support, both physically and mentally. His eyes travel down my body at a turtle's pace, landing mid-thigh where my dress ends.

"I want to see your legs as I rub them this time," he says as he brings one arm between our legs, his hand sliding up my dress to my upper thigh. He grabs it, causing my head to fall back with a close-lipped moan.

"You can't..." My words are lost to the sensation of him squeezing my thigh while one of his fingers skims the outline of my panties over my heated pussy. I detest the fact that we have way too much clothes on.

"You *loved* that we were surrounded by people," he says with a smug look. "I consider myself a decent reader of people, Kate. You were *so* into it."

The denial is on my tongue, but the drop in my gut tells me he was right. Beneath all the worry and fear, was the insane amount of excitement his hidden touches brought me.

"If you want to blame me, to tell me I'm a bad influence, go for it. But I know the truth. I know I can't make people feel what's not in them."

My jaw goes slack at his words, because I've never looked at it that way. His hand glides to my other thigh, his fingers brushing past my clit, exposed through my lips purely because of how wet I am. I inhale sharply and his stupid, sexy smirk tells me that his touch was no accident.

This guy must have way more experience than me, making me feel so insecure. I don't think I could even find his dick right now without using my eyes, and he's expertly groping me without breaking eye contact.

"What's that brain of yours worrying about now?" he asks, moving my panties aside before slipping a finger into my soaking pussy. He slides right in and I forget his words, thrusting my hips into his hand. His thumb moves up, shoving my panties all the way over and gliding so freaking slowly over my clit.

"Kate." His words are a slow drawl, and when I don't respond immediately, he stops moving his fingers. I still feel them hovering over my aching pussy, but the lack of movement helps me recover my thoughts.

"I... don't want to talk about it right now." I can't confess my insecurities to him while he's doing these things to me. I may not be an expert at hookups, but I know damn well bringing up other women he's been intimate with is probably—no, *definitely*—a turnoff.

"Do you want me to stop?" I'm surprised at the hint of worry I hear in his tone. My eyes meet his and the hesitation I see in them causes me to close my eyes.

"No," I reply, wiggling my hips so I rub myself on his fingers. I can just *feel* the smirk overtaking his face, and his thumb resumes its small circles. I sigh in relief and continue to grind myself on him.

"Thank fuck," he groans. His lips find mine and I grant him immediate access, our tongues swirling together. His taste is all I ever want to know. I bring my hand to his jaw and grasp, pulling him closer. I feel his lips tilt up and he slows the pace of his tongue and finger.

"You're a greedy one, aren't you?" he murmurs against my lips. I buck my hips in response and he thrusts two fingers into my pussy. When I moan, he swallows it with his mouth. His lips over mine are intoxicating, and his fingers inside me have me seeing stars.

Char was right, I do need this.

Still, I hardly recognize myself. The way my body is reacting to him is foreign to me. I don't even know his last name, and he's got me showing parts of myself I've exposed to few.

"I'm going to need you to talk to me, princess," he says, pulling back and watching his fingers pumping in and out of me at the perfect pace.

"That…" I'm nervous to be so intimate with someone I hardly know. Am I supposed to just say what I'm feeling? Do I act like my normal, sexual self? "That feels—"

My throat catches when I hear a door open down the hall.

Chapter Five

December 23rd

"This is Ryan's room. He's at his grandparents' for the night."

My eyes widen at the sound of Rowan's voice. My eyes lock on Lorenzo's equally surprised look, but his are missing the terror I feel. He pulls his fingers out of me and brings the index finger to his lips, telling me to keep quiet.

"*Obviously,*" I mouth.

Then, my jaw drops when he licks both fingers clean.

It takes every ounce of willpower I have not to audibly react to *that*. He quietly scoots off the bed and motions for me to join him. He opens the closet and nods for me to enter first.

He's about to take a step in when he looks back and dashes to the door. He turns the lock, my anxiety shooting sky high with the idea of Rowan walking in here. And finding us. My throat constricts, panic overtaking me.

Lorenzo joins me, slowly and soundlessly closing the door. Thankfully, there's nothing in here except for a box in the corner. My heart feels as though it will beat out of my chest. I try to see how Lorenzo is handling this, but it's too dark to make anything out.

My eyes finally adjust as I hear light footsteps in the neighboring room. A muffled voice speaks, but I can't make out who it belongs to. Hell, I might not even know who that is. The door snaps shut and I let out a breath before inhaling and holding.

We're the next room up, if they plan on seeing it. I didn't even look at the bed to make sure we didn't leave any evidence. My hands are clammy and my heart hasn't settled in the least bit.

I nearly scream when Lorenzo's hands land on my waist and he pulls me to him. My back is to his front, and he squeezes me in what I assume is reassurance. That's what I'm needing, at least.

He places a gentle kiss atop my head, reminiscent of the one he placed after I'd assaulted my ex. It feels like too much for what he's claiming this is, but there's no time to think about that now.

My senses are heightened, trying to pick up any noise that indicates they're coming this way. I hear footsteps, but I can't tell if they're getting closer or farther away. I've never had any experience with this, why the hell should I know?!

Lorenzo squeezes me again, and the door opens. A second later, the light switch flips on. I lean up to look at Lorenzo as Rowan speaks.

"This is the guest bedroom, which is where it's all usually at."

Where what's at?

"Moved it for the party?" an unrecognizable male voice says.

Not that I give too much thought into who it is. No, I'm distracted with the look on Lorenzo's face. Now that my eyes have adjusted to the dark and the light is peeking in through the cracks in the bi-fold doors, I see the humor etched into his face. His dimples are deepened and his eyebrows are raised as though we're watching a movie and not hiding in the closet of our boss's house. If he wouldn't be heard, I'm certain he'd be snickering.

I'm hooking up with a loon.

"Yeah, yeah," Rowan replies. "Can't have..." His voice floats away when I hear the door shut, silently killing me because the light was left on. I pray that they return downstairs and don't go down the hallway extending past Rowan's room. It wraps around the living room, so they'd have to come back this way to go downstairs.

Rowan's words are muffled, and I'd likely be able to make them out if I focused, but I have a more pertinent issue to deal with. I turn and rip Lorenzo's hands off of me.

"We're done!" I whisper in the lowest voice I can use. He's staring at my mouth, probably trying to figure out what the hell I just said.

He brings a finger to his lips, shushing me. The image of him cleaning me off of him just moments ago has me wanting to feel him again, which irks me more. I cross my arms and huff, then remember I need to keep silent when his smile falters and he gives me a serious look. I hold my breath and don't move a centimeter as I keep my ears peeled.

"About five years," Rowan replies. I think his voice is closer to us, but I can't be sure. I continue to listen to the footsteps, and when I'm certain they're walking back down the stairs, I pull open the closet with less care than I should exercise. I'm fixing my dress as Lorenzo steps out.

"I'm leaving," I say. With the lights left on and the near heart attack I've suffered, my voice of reason is all I can hear.

"Come on, what are the chances he comes back up here *again*?"

Is he serious? "What about his wife, or a party straggler?! You are out of your mind, really. I—"

"How did you get into finance?"

His question throws me. "Huh?"

"Let's just talk. We're allowed to talk up here."

Talk? He's confusing the hell out of me. We're supposed to be hooking up and then never speaking of any of this again. Even *that* is something I don't want to do anymore. This was stupid and I should have listened to reason from the start.

"Why would we be talking upstairs? Lorenzo, I'm sorry, but I have to go. This is the stupidest thing I've ever done, and I mean that literally."

If I didn't know any better, I would think that I saw hurt flash in his eyes. But I certainly imagined it, because there is only humor there now.

"To get away from the noise, is one obvious reason," he muses. "To discuss how you're going to pay for my car repairs is another."

I very uncharacteristically swat his arm. "Stop!" But I can't help the giggles that escape me.

What is it about this man that has me acting like someone else? *Feeling* like someone else?

Lorenzo sits at the edge of the bed and pats the spot next to him. I sit, though I'm not sure why. I honestly feel insane right now.

"So?" he presses. The change in gears is making my head spin.

"Um, well, I studied finance in college. Numbers have always made sense to me. They're factual; logical."

He nods his head in understanding. "How did you start working for Rowan?"

"I started as an intern when I was in my third year of college," I explain. Lorenzo loops one of my curls in his finger, but I continue. "As soon as I graduated, he offered me a full time position as an underwriter. He's great."

"What's your last name?" Lorenzo's other hand has started drawing circles on the leg closest to him, distracting me.

"Appleton."

"Are you from Azalea Pines?" He trails his fingers up my leg, and I squirm in response.

"Y-yes."

"How old is Felix?" He's still stroking me and looping his finger around my curl.

"Seven."

"Any siblings?"

I mumble my response incoherently.

"What was that?" he asks, his voice filled with seduction. I suck in a breath when he releases my hair and runs the finger down my jaw, neck, and collarbone, settling just above my breast. His fingers start painting across my chest and I press my back into them, wanting to feel his touch through my suddenly too thick bra.

My lips part and Lorenzo stares at them, biting down on his lower lip. It makes me feral.

There's no way Rowan would come up here a second time, would he?

"Kate?" I meet his hooded gaze with my own. The logical part of my brain is shouting again, telling me to quit succumbing to his games.

"You don't actually care about these answers, do you?" I ask with an attempt at sounding suspicious.

"Numbers. Appleton. Felix. Seven." His face comes closer to mine. I feel his hot breath over my lips, causing them to press together. "Couldn't catch that last response, though."

I know what he's doing, but I can't bring myself to stop him. My core clenches as he finally palms my breast, my nipples pebbling against the smooth fabric of my undergarment. I bring my hand over his and squeeze, my eyes fluttering shut with a moan.

"Mmm," he whispers in pure lust. He slides his fingers under my dress, the anticipation in my chest growing. Being the smug asshole that he is, he doesn't touch me where I need him to. Instead, he continues those circles on my inner thigh right *next* to my pussy, causing my desire to grow exponentially.

But with it, my frustration grows, fueling my boldness. I reach out and find him bulging into his slacks. My tentative fingers start stroking but his groans urge me to keep going.

"Lay down," he commands. My body retracts before I can tell it not to.

"I know what you're doing," I tell him, peering up at him through my lashes.

"I want to fuck you now," he breathes. He lays on his side next to me, propping himself up on his elbow. "And I know you want me to."

I want to deny it, to tell him that he's a cocky asshole that knows nothing about me. But I did lay down, didn't I? And I can't ignore his hand on my upper thigh or his fingers toying with my panty line.

"Why did you ask me about boundaries?" I blurt out, feeling suddenly nervous at the recollection of his question.

His fingers stop moving. "I always ask that. I want you to be comfortable."

Always. As in, he does this all the time.

"Rowan's not going to come up here a second time," he says, misreading my silence. I let him, nodding my head.

I bring my hand to his shirt, opening the first button with shaky fingers, my nerves on display. This is the first time I'm having sex for well over a year, and I have no clue what to expect. He kicks off his shoes and I move to the second button.

"Tear it off," he murmurs, one finger *finally* slipping through my panties and traveling down my center. It glides smoothly thanks to the near swimming pool of desire waiting there for him. He groans and glides over my opening, then back up, landing on my clit.

My back arches, my hips lifting off the bed. He hikes my dress up with his free hand and stares at his finger working on my pussy.

I move my fingers to his next button. "You're going to need your shirt after."

"Fuck the shirt," he growls, his eyes fixated on what he's doing to me. I ignore him, moving my fingers down to each button, unclasping them to reveal his body to me.

I stare as shamelessly as he's been staring at me, admiring what I can see of his toned chest. When he increases the pressure on my clit, I moan and watch his abdomen contract.

"Do you trust me?" he asks. If I wasn't clouded by all the oxytocin released from my brain, I'd laugh at him.

"Absolutely not."

His finger stops moving and I circle my hips, begging him to continue. "At least for this moment?"

I'm not sure if it's driven by honesty or need, but I tell him yes. He pulls at my dress and I lift up so he can peel it off, leaving me in my bra and underwear. His eyes slowly sweep over my body. When they reach my panties, I squirm under his scrutiny, causing his eyes to jump to mine.

"You're so sexy, Kate," he says. He constantly knows where my mind goes. It feels like there's a strange tether of connection between us, but how could that be? We don't know each other. He said he's good at reading people, so maybe it's just that.

"You, too," I respond. *Is that appropriate to say to a guy?*

He gives me an earnest smile, removing my doubt. He shrugs out of his dress shirt, revealing his full upper body to me. He has an all black tattoo on his upper chest, near his shoulder. It's some sort of spiral with a thick, bold star in the center.

He brings his face to mine, hovering over me. His eyes take in my lips before locking with my gaze. The intensity I find sends shocks throughout my entire body. It feels palpable, real, like it has a life of its own.

I can't help that my stupid heart is about to beat out of my chest. If I didn't know in the back of my mind that this is just a hookup, I'd be falling so fast.

He brings his lips to mine and I melt into it, my hand looping around his neck and pulling him closer. This kiss is different, slower and seductive. Our mouths move in sync and when he teases my lips with the tip of his tongue, I breathe into him before bringing my tongue to meet his.

We continue kissing like this, the feelings deepening and expanding. We go from slow and seductive to passionate and needy. It feels like this is more. It feels like I want more.

Once we're breathless, he pulls back, the cinnamon and smoke tickling my nose. He reaches over my head and grabs one of the fluffy pillows from the perfectly made bed. When he pulls the pillowcase off, my eyebrows pinch together.

"I want to do so many things to you, Kate." He folds up the pillowcase until it's a long rectangle, almost like a—

"Turn around." I meet his hooded gaze in confusion. He bites his lower lip and tugs on the pillowcase, pulling it taut.

I want to question him, but I don't want to appear clueless. So, I do as he says and turn around. My butt is exposed, the lace riding up my cheeks so they're only half hidden. When he doesn't move, I crane my neck to look at him.

His eyelids are even lower, staring at my ass. I blush, equally enthralled and timid that I turn him on. He stands up, and I let my head drop onto the bed with my face turned to the side.

Now that I'm not looking at him and I hear him unbuttoning his pants, the apprehension and nerves take over. What is he planning to do? Do I just lay here?

I hear a door open and my head shoots up, but the bedroom door is shut. I turn my head towards the closet and find Lorenzo pulling out the box that was in the corner. He's in black boxer briefs that hug his dick in the most appealing way. His strong legs are flexed as he comes back to the bed.

I'm about to tell him to lock the door when he moves towards it, proving that we're somehow on the same wavelength. After locking the door, he prowls toward me and places the box next to my thighs.

I didn't realize before that it's a set of Christmas lights. When he catches me looking, he gently pushes my head onto the bed with the hand that has the pillowcase in it.

"Close your eyes," he says, and for some strange reason, I do.

He brushes the curl off my face and tucks it behind my ear. Then, my nose feels the tickle of fabric before it's over my eyes and I'm enveloped in darkness. I feel Lorenzo's body brush over my legs as he leans to tie the pillowcase behind my head. He tightens the knot, applying pressure to the bridge of my nose.

My heart is going to beat out of my chest, I know it. I don't consider myself a prude by any means, but I've never been blindfolded before. And with someone I don't know? This feels too out of control.

But, like with everything else when I'm around this man, I don't stop it.

"Lift up," Lorenzo says, sounding farther away. It goes even darker when I hear a click, the minimal light under the blindfold disappearing. I use my hands to lift me up and bring my knees under my hips, but Lorenzo chuckles.

His hand presses into the small of my back. "Only your hips, baby."

Baby?

I lower my head down and bring my hands to the side of my body. My breasts press into the mattress, my butt open but only partially exposed for him, due to the underwear.

I feel his fingers graze my spine before he unclasps my bra. It falls by the sides of my triceps, and I lift my arms to remove it.

"Don't move." I stop immediately. A light sheen of sweat is covering my body with the nerves coming over me.

His fingers brush my waist, then my hips, before looping through my panties and pulling them down. I move my leg so he can pull them all the way off but his palm meets my thigh and stops it.

"I'm going to make this really easy for you. Don't do anything unless I tell you to."

I'm not sure why that phrasing snaps me out of my catatonic state, but it does.

"You're just going to boss me around?" I turn my head on instinct but I'm blinded by the fabric tied to my head.

"For play, yes. Unless you tell me that you're not okay with it." His tone is serious, the silk and smoke nowhere to be heard.

For play. I feel the resistance in me dripping away, wanting to know what he means by that. What's the worst that could happen?

"Talk to me, Kate."

"Okay." I move my head back to where it was.

"I want you to keep all this lace on." I nod my head, my cheek rubbing against the sheets.

"I'm going to make good use of these Christmas lights."

That sets me on edge again. "What, like tie my hands up?" *Won't they be too long?*

He chuckles but doesn't respond. I resist the urge to demand he explain what he's doing. *I can do this, I can go with the flow for one night.*

I hear him digging in the box, the lightbulbs rattling against the cardboard. I wish I had read the length they are so I at least know what we're working with here.

The box clatters to the ground and the lights brush my calf as he drops them in place on the bed. His warm finger slides down my pussy, still soaked with desire. I shift my weight back, leaning into his touch.

"I love how ready you are for me," he says, stroking my exposed ass. His voice has reverted to silk, and I just want to hear it on replay. When I hear shuffling, I assume he must be removing his boxers.

After more shuffling, the sound of tearing makes me realize three things. One: he's tearing open a condom. Two: I didn't even think about protection. Three: this is actually happening.

My pussy tightens with the last realization and my nipples harden, brushing against the sheet. There's a moment of silence before his hands grasp my cheeks, squeezing and stroking.

"Something tells me you need me to start slowly," he says. That sounds like a challenge, and I want to tell him to do whatever he wants; that I can handle it. But I'm honestly not sure if that's true, so I keep my mouth shut.

His dick lines up at my entrance and I inhale a breath full of anticipation. His hands glide up to my hips and grip tightly, then pull me onto him. As he enters, I hold my breath.

And then the feeling of euphoria takes over. If it's my year's dry spell or him, I don't know, and I don't want to figure it out. I just want to feel him deep inside me. I tighten over him and hold in my moan, some part of my brain still remembering that we need to stay quiet.

"You feel so fucking good, Kate," he says, lust dripping from every syllable. He stays still for a moment, his hard cock throbbing and teasing me. I squirm my hips, unable to resist asking him for more. He grips my hips harder at that, his nails digging into my skin.

Rather than pulling out and giving me what I need, he brings one of his hands to my clit and starts rubbing it. My blinded eyes roll into the back of my head and I'm actually grateful we're not in missionary position. I'm not sure that I would let myself be this vulnerable.

"That feels good, doesn't it?"

"Mmhmm," I half speak, half moan.

Then he pinches my clit and I shove my head into the mattress to stifle my scream.

"Shhh," he soothes, and I find that it actually feels... *good*. Not terrifying, the way it probably should feel when he's in control like this.

"I want to provide you with pleasure. I do. But you have to be a good girl. And good girls earn it. So stop being a bad girl and show me just how *good* you can be."

He resumes rubbing my clit and the sensation is ten times more intense after his assault. I moan into the mattress, too overcome with pleasure to move my head to the side for air. He stands up, his hand returning to my hip, and he withdraws his dick.

He slides in and out at an even pace, my pussy tightening and getting wetter than I can ever remember it being. It feels so good and I want more so desperately, but I force myself to focus on not moving a millimeter. He gradually increases the pace and I start to pant with the oncoming orgasm.

And then, he stops. He pulls all the way out of me, leaving me cold and exposed and frenzied. I let out my second whimper of the night, feeling as pathetic as I did the first time. But if it gets him to thrust back into me, I won't regret it.

"We need to be quiet, remember, baby?"

I nod my head, but who knows if he can see it. I turn my face to the side to catch a deep breath of air now that some of my brain cells are functioning with the lack of him.

I hear a rustling and he says, "Lift your head."

I do, my neck straining with the euphoria floating through me and the wish to just let it take me. I hear movement on either side of my face before something is placed around my neck. A piece of it pokes me, and I realize it's the Christmas lights.

The tension on the cord I feel a moment later tells me he's pulling. I let my neck angle further back, and he wraps another strand around, doubling on the pressure. He pulls tighter, but my neck can't shift any more, which restricts my airflow even more.

"This should help." I can hear his grin and I'm sure he's proud of himself. I'm at his mercy and I should be more frightened. But right now, I just want him back inside me so I can come.

I get exactly what I wish for, though in a much rougher way. He thrusts back into me with excruciating force, causing my face to fall towards the mattress. But it only moves a few inches due to the cord pulling on my neck like horse reigns, my ability to breathe nearly non-existent.

He pounds into me and I can hardly catch my breath. I move my arms to hold me up, the bra straps straining as they pull apart. My hands clench the bed sheets as I swallow my moans. But then he stops again, this time with his dick deep inside me. I try to whimper pathetically a third time, but no sound comes out and now I really can't breathe.

I'm seeing stars as my face burns with the rush of blood. I find it ironic that he made me keep quiet yet the sound of his palm hitting my ass reverberates around the room. "Back down," he hisses, and it actually sounds like he's angry.

I shift to my elbows, and he pulls on the cord. I put my arms down on the bed, and he loosens his hold before thrusting into me again. He grabs one of my hips, moving me to meet him at every thrust.

"That's a good fucking girl. Just look at this, you taking me so well. I knew you'd be wild for this."

I am wild. I'm out of my goddamn mind with his movements and the restriction of air. I'm afraid I might actually pass out, but the building climax doesn't let me care. As soon as I think that I'd like to rub myself to help him push me over the edge, he takes his hand off my hip and circles around, rubbing my clit vigorously. The cord loosened with his movement so I take in a strangled breath through my mouth.

"That's it, come for me baby," he says. "Give it to me."

My body explodes, the orgasm starting in my core and shooting out. My body gives, but he pulls on the cord and I can't collapse like I want to. He thrusts even faster, even harder, and my orgasm crescendos when he follows me into the rubble of my explosion.

When he lets go of the cords, the strands fall onto my back and I collapse into the mattress. I can feel that my breath is erratic, but I'm comforted when I hear that his matches.

We stay just like that for a few moments, bringing our bodies down to earth and our breaths back to normal. When he pulls out of me, I feel the loss not just in my pussy, but in my chest.

He collapses on the bed next to me, and I turn to look at him. But I see nothing, because the pillowcase is still blocking my sight. Lorenzo chuckles before he unties the knot at the back of my head, letting it drop onto the bed in front of me.

Our eyes lock instantly, and I search his for... something. I'm afraid to name what. It seems like he's searching mine with the same intensity, and my heart speeds up despite my settling breath.

"That was..." he starts.

"Fun?"

He smirks. "*Very*."

It's too dark for me to see if there's a twinkle in his eyes. As my orgasm floats away, I become more aware of the physical world around me. My ass is covered in goosebumps from the mixture of sweat and cold air now that his body isn't touching it. I shift my hips and take in Lorenzo's naked body, his shoulders lean and broad.

I stare at his tattoo again, then roam lower to his chest and abdomen, soaking it all in. I want to memorize the man who gave me the best orgasm of my life.

The music downstairs changes, and I jump onto my hands. The string of lights fall off my back and I pull them off my neck.

"Shit! We need to get dressed," I whisper, the reminder of the party—and more importantly, where it is—causing panic to flood me.

"No one's coming, princess," he murmurs, resting lazily on the bed. Ignoring him, I jump off and pull my panties up, then fix my bra. Locating my dress, I toss it on.

"You can do whatever you want, but I'm leaving." I can't think past the rush to get out of here. I need to get back to safety, where I can't be caught doing things I shouldn't be.

For more reasons than one.

"I'm going, I'm going," he says in a mock irritated voice while he scoots off the bed. He picks up his boxers and pants, pulling them on. "You know, I think I like you better with my cock inside you and that cord around your neck."

Ouch. I grab his shirt and toss it to him, then shake out the pillowcase and put the pillow back in it. As I place it meticulously on the bed, trying to remember exactly how it looked, Lorenzo pulls on my arm.

"I'm only joking." He stares at me until I meet his gaze, and I see nothing but sincerity. I break the contact and finish replacing the pillow, then glance down at my feet.

In all the excitement, I didn't even realize my heels were on the whole time. Lorenzo sits on the bed to put his shoes back on, and I stand awkwardly to the side of the bed.

"I'll go out first, so there's no suspicion," I say, jumping into strategy.

"It'll be fine, no one's going to notice. I can drive you home."

"Oh. Okay," I say, feeling like his words are a dismissal.

"Unless you don't want to return to Felix and Friends?"

It does silly things to my heart that he remembers what I wanted. "Yeah, I do. Thanks."

He smiles, and I force myself to look away so the dumb part of me that is prepared to fall head over heels for this guy won't. Once his shoes are back on, he takes my face in his hands and places a featherlight kiss on my forehead.

He pulls away before I can react, opening the bedroom door and holding it open for me. I scan the room one last time, then rush to put the lights back into the box and return them to the closet. I give Lorenzo a stern look but he only shrugs, as if leaving evidence won't do anything to implicate us.

I stomp out of the room, then force myself to stop because we need to be quiet. We travel down the stairs and I head straight for the exit, refusing to psych myself out by looking at the party. It seems to be in full swing, an electronic dance version of "Grandma Got Run Over

By A Reindeer" blaring through the speakers, mixing with the sound of talk and laughter.

The cold air whips at my skin when I open the door, but I hurry down the porch steps to the lawn. All the cars are parked along the street, and I have no idea what car belongs to Lorenzo. He comes out of the house a moment later, sidling up next to me.

"The black Audi down there is mine." My eyes follow his finger pointing to an all black, two door Audi A5. The tints are black, the rims are black, even the headlights seem to be covered with a tinted plate. The car shines under the street light, looking as though it was freshly waxed today. My mouth falls open but I quickly shut it due to the frigid temperature.

I've never looked at the payroll, but I know more or less how much people make at our company. He should *not* be able to afford that. He must come from an influential family or something.

He unlocks the car with his key fob and pads over, the headlights beaming. Thinking it's the least he could do after our escapade tonight, I'm offended when he doesn't rush to open my door. I get inside and shut the door quickly to hide from the cold and my hurt. Maybe I should have gotten in the backseat if I'm so meaningless to him.

A few moments later, I hear the trunk slam and turn around to see him circling the car to the driver's side.

"Thought you could use this," he says, handing me a black leather jacket. He puts the key fob into the cupholder and presses the push to start button, saving me the embarrassment of being caught with my mouth hanging.

I tug the jacket on, appreciating the immediate warmth it provides me. It has *his* smell on it, and I try my best not to inhale it deeply over and over again.

"You're not in the habit of giving thanks, are you?" Lorenzo asks as he peers out of his window and peels onto the road. He floors the gas and I throw my arms out to grip the door and console.

Lorenzo either doesn't notice or ignores my fearful position. He hardly slows down at the stop sign before barreling down the road.

"Don't you need to know where I live?" I ask, forcing my hands to release their tense hold on the car. But he continues to drive at high speed, and I lose my temper. "Can you slow down?"

He glances over at me, which causes me more panic since his eyes are off the road for far longer than necessary. He must sense it, because his foot lets off the accelerator. I let out a breath and he grins. I roll my eyes and stare out the window.

"Where do you live?" he asks, making a left onto the main road of our town.

"If you give me your phone, I'll put in the address," I respond. The last thing he needs to be doing is typing while driving.

"Just tell me," he says. I eye him for a moment and then rattle off the address. He guns the gas again, turning at the appropriate street towards my apartment complex.

My dad's always said you can learn a lot from a person by the way they drive. I don't think I like what Lorenzo is telling me right now.

The rest of the ride is spent in silence, save for the roar of his engine, the wind whipping at the car, and my heartbeat in my ears. At some point, the seat heaters turned on and warmed me enough that his jacket almost felt stifling. But I kept it on, liking the feel of him over me, even indirectly.

I should probably explore *why* I like it, but I'll save that for another time. Or maybe I'll just ignore it forever. Lorenzo keeps his eyes trained on the road and plays no music. He swerves in and out of lanes, treating our streets like his own personal race car video game.

I try to distract myself from the potential threat of death by inconspicuously glancing around his car. The back seat is littered with used cups, clothing, and other junk I can't fully make out. Obviously I don't own a car, but if I did, I know I'd keep it spotless.

The street lights are whizzing past us, so I glance at the dashboard and nearly choke on my own spit. "You're going 70 miles per hour!"

He glances over at me again and I point to the road. He laughs but turns back to the windshield. "Yeah, you said to slow down."

"Slow down? The speed limit is 45! Do you have a death wish?"

"I'm not afraid of death." Before I can retaliate—because being afraid of death and wanting death are two totally different things—he breaks hard and pulls up to my complex a moment later. I didn't even realize we were close.

As soon as he throws the car into park, I unclick my seatbelt and open the door, desperate for the stable ground and the safety of my apartment. I slam the door shut and turn to the sidewalk, but I hear the window open.

"My jacket, princess?" *Oh, right.* I shrug out of it and drop it onto the seat I vacated, then meet his stare. Remembering his comment about gratitude, I decide I should probably thank him.

"Thanks for the ride, and the, uh, jacket," I say tersely. I'm not sure how the energy between us changed so drastically. From the way he was looking at me after sex to... this strange distance. If my orgasm hadn't been so intense, I'd be questioning whether I made it all up in my head.

"Of course. I had fun tonight."

"Me, too."

A moment of awkward silence passes. Well, awkward for me. Lorenzo looks completely comfortable, giving me a lopsided grin.

"See ya Wednesday."

He peels off before I can wish him Happy Holidays.

Chapter Six

December 24th

"He called you a brat?" Char's astonished voice blares through the speaker phone as I fold and put away my laundry. "That's... kinda hot."

"It's really not," I reply, hanging tonight's dress in its place in my closet. Yes, I'm folding laundry at 3 am. Yes, I already washed the dress I wore. I'm filling Char in on all the Lorenzo details, because my mind has been swarming with thoughts of him since I returned home. I finish telling her everything that happened and she whistles.

"Well, it sounds like it had to be just a *little* hot if you ended up fucking him in your boss's place!"

Maybe it didn't piss me off the way it should, but no way in hell I'm admitting that to her. "So what am I supposed to do?"

"It doesn't sound like there's anything *to* do. He made it clear it was just for fun."

"Right. But how do I handle seeing him at work?"

"Just treat him like any other coworker. That's what he is."

Right... just a coworker I slept with and haven't been able to stop thinking about. Maybe that's just because it's so recent and new. I mean, it literally just happened. This should pass as the days go by. I'm determined to stay away from guys, at least for the foreseeable future. It seems as though I can't stay away from fuckboys, and I need a detox.

Even if I was going to keep dating, Lorenzo would not be it. I mean, he's arrogant, for starters. He probably doesn't like to do any of the things I like. The only reason he even had an interest in me is because he met me doing something crazy. I still can't fully fathom the fact that I did punch and knee Trent.

"Kaaate." Char's sing-song voice breaks my train of thought.

"Sorry, what was that?" I finish folding the last articles of clothing and begin putting them into their drawers.

"I said, I'm so proud of you! You stood up for yourself with Trent and then you had a one night stand! I thought this day would never come."

"Is that really something to be *proud* of?" She didn't even say she was proud of me when I was offered the job with Rowan.

"Absolutely! Just telling Trent to fuck off was a huge step, but then you punched him? Lorenzo's right, it really is badass."

"I crotch-splotched him, too," I say with a wide grin. *I wonder what Lorenzo is doing right now.*

No. We're not doing this.

"Exactly! Now, you can go back to being Regular Kate, with these memories to remind you who you could be if you wanted to."

"I like who I am."

"I *love* who you are, Kate. Obviously. That's why I'm your BFF." I smile and listen as she proceeds to tell me about the date she had last night.

Char and I became friends in elementary school, when who you are isn't defined by your choices in life and your personality isn't strong enough to clash. I really think if we met now, we'd never click. We're about as polar opposite as it gets, but in a lot of ways, it works.

She's the yin to my yang. I ground her, and she helps me ride the waves.

"We need to get some sleep," I say, putting my laundry hamper in the corner of my closet.

"I'll sleep when I'm dead. I'm going to catch up on some reading before I call it. See ya at 10:30."

Maybe we would be friends even if we met now; we do share a love for reading. Then again, she reads romance and I stick to non-fiction.

"Char, tomorrow is Christmas Eve. I'm going to my parents' house."

I call Felix over from the chair in front of my desk. He stretches before leaping off, then struts to my bed. He waits for me to lay on it before he jumps up, snuggling next to my head on the pillow.

"Why does that mean we can't brunch first?"

I roll my eyes but tell her I'm not going. I've already wrapped my presents but I'd like to get ready and head to my parents house early. They live about twenty minutes from me, but we don't see each other all that often. I talk to my mom regularly through text or phone, but we're both introverted homebodies. Dad drives cargo trucks for a living, so he's gone often.

After we hang up, I plug my phone into the charger and place it on my nightstand, then turn off the lamp. Once I'm settled into my white, cotton sheets, I close my eyes to let sleep take me.

Within minutes, I know that's not happening. My mind is racing with the memories of just a few hours earlier.

I don't even know his last name. I'm sure I'll find out Wednesday, but my need-to-know-everything brain wants to know now. I grab my phone, convincing myself that I deserve to know who I just slept with. I search his first name on social media, but thousands of results populate. Lorenzo isn't *that* uncommon of a name.

I try searching with our city name, but none of the photos that populate are of him. Instead, I pull up the company's page. Maybe

Lorenzo started following it, or he does know someone that works there. I type Lorenzo into various searches and skim through people's profiles, but I come up empty.

I should have asked him his last name. He asked mine. Giving up, I place my phone back on the nightstand, deciding against digging deeper. Come Wednesday, I'll get his last name from the company directory and look him up then. Or, maybe I won't. He's just a coworker, right?

Then again, I have looked into some other coworkers. I get curious, and the internet can often reveal things about people they'd never come out and tell you.

I close my eyes again, but my mind races with thoughts of what seeing him at work will be like. Do I say hello? What if he ignores me? Are we supposed to be friendlier now that we've had sex? What if he does tell people what we did?

Eventually, I fall into a restless sleep.

Chapter Seven

December 27th

"I didn't see you leave the party Saturday," Victor says, holding a steaming mug of coffee in his hand. My heart starts racing as I formulate a response.

"Yeah, I left around 9:30. Had to check on Felix," I reply with an awkward chuckle.

"It got pretty wild after midnight. That new guy was passing out shots and being like, the ultimate hype man."

"Lorenzo?" I say before I can stop myself. *He went back after dropping me off?*

"Yeah, the one you introduced us to."

"Oh." Victor gives me a curious look but I turn back to my computer screen. "Well, I'm glad it was fun. Too bad I missed it."

"How was your Christmas?" he asks.

"Pretty good." I should ask him about his, but my mind is reeling with the information he dropped.

"I'll let you get back to work, see you for lunch," Victor says when I start moving my mouse. Aimlessly, but he doesn't know that.

I thought he was going home. Why did he offer to drive me if he wanted to stay at the party?

I open the company directory and search for his name, but it hasn't been added yet. Frustration bubbles in me for various reasons.

I shouldn't have slept with him. I knew it was stupid, but I couldn't stop myself. His attractiveness hooked me and his personality reeled me in. And now, I'm the idiot fish out of water that's going to be cooked for dinner.

I push it to the back of my mind and focus on my work. No one will know about it, and I will be denying it from here moving forward. I focus on reviewing the schedule Jasmine forwarded me. Numbers, I can deal with.

• • • ● ● • ● ● • • •

At noon sharp, I lock my computer and head to the small break room where most of us eat lunch. There's a few restaurants nearby, but we only get thirty minutes, which I'm actually grateful for. I don't need an hour to eat, forcing me to be at work later.

I pull my packed lunch from the refrigerator and sit between Victor and Alexandra, who've already got their leftovers out. We engage in small talk as I lay out my turkey sandwich, apple, carrots, and hummus.

Before I can process why I do it, my head turns towards the opening to the break room and my breath hitches. There he is, in all black, with the familiar look of amusement. He even kept his eyebrow piercing in, although it's not like Rowan would care in the slightest.

His eyes shift to mine but I avert my gaze, lifting my sandwich and taking a bite. No matter how many times Char told me to "treat him like any other coworker," I have no idea how to actually do that. Images of the wall I stared at as he thrust into me with the lights pulling on my throat cloud my vision, and my cheeks heat.

"Hey, Lorenzo," Alexandra says. *Don't look up, don't look up.*

"Alexandra, Kate, Victor," he says. His voice causes my stomach to swoop. I need to look up, knowing it's attention grabbing if I don't. When I raise my head, his eyes shift from Alexandra to me, but he moves them just as quickly to Victor.

I should be grateful that he's acting so normally, treating me exactly like the other coworkers. But the stupid girl in me feels disappointed that that's really all I am.

"There he is! How's your first day treating you?" Victor says from my right. I swallow and take a sip of my water, willing it to assuage my nerves.

"Feels like I've worked here my whole life." His eyes land on mine. "We missed you for the rest of the party, Kate. How was Felix?"

"Oh, um"—I wipe my face with a napkin and clear my throat—"he was happy to have me home."

"I started telling her about how wild the party got. Rowan's the best boss ever, letting shit like that happen at his house. When you took that body shot"—My eyes shoot to Lorenzo but his expression doesn't falter as he listens to Victor with a grin—"off Sara, I swore he would shut the whole thing down. But then he started cheering you on and I was done for."

Lorenzo laughs and responds, but I can't hear him through the horror I feel. My stomach rolls and I completely lose my appetite. So not only did he return to the party, but he was taking shots off another woman? Did he have sex with her, too?

I feel dumber than a rock. He made it clear what it was, but obviously I'm a fool and incapable of leaving it there. He owes me nothing. I'm ashamed at how let down I feel. When he walks away, I'll put my food back and go to my desk. I need to process this alone.

"I'm gonna grab my lunch and sit with some of the guys from my department. Catch ya later." Lorenzo dismisses himself without looking at me again.

I start packing up my lunch and say, "I just realized I forgot to do something. I'm going back to my desk."

"You work too hard," Alexandra says between bites of food.

"It makes her happy," Victor says with a shrug. More of our coworkers are filtering into the break room, making the space feel cramped and suffocating. I stand up and wave goodbye, forgoing returning my food to the fridge. I'll just keep it at my desk so if anyone sees me, they'll believe I'm working through lunch.

Once I'm back at my desk, I allow myself a small moment to fall apart. I feel like a fool and I can't even blame him. I knew what it was. I thought I was okay with it. But obviously, I'm not.

I pull out my phone to text Char, but I don't even know what to say. How do I explain that I'm a hopeless romantic idiot who regrets what I did? Especially after she was so "proud"?

"So, this is where the magic happens?" My phone clatters to the floor when I hear Lorenzo's voice. He retrieves it and hands it to me, his brow arched in amusement.

And it pisses me the hell off.

"I have work to do," I tell him, putting my phone on my desk and staring at the computer screen. I input my password and open my emails.

"Are you okay?" He has the audacity to sound concerned.

"Never better." I refuse to make eye contact with him. I'm not exactly treating him like a coworker, but fuck him.

"Hey." When I click on an email and don't respond or look at him, his finger tugs at my chin, forcing me to look at him. I immediately glance around to check that the office is empty. Confirming we're alone, I turn back to him.

He's leaning against my desk and staring at me intently. Smoke and cinnamon drift over when he speaks. "I told you I'd keep the secret."

What, so that's what all this was? Him keeping the secret?

It doesn't matter.

"Yes, thank you." I force myself to sound calm and collected.

"Is this the *real* Kate, then?"

My eyes narrow but he doesn't waver. "This is the *only* Kate. Now if you'll excuse me, I do have some things to take care of."

I force my eyes to stare at my computer screen, because really I just want to take him all in. His smell, his voice, his presence in my space... it's causing me to want more.

"See ya, princess."

Chapter Eight

December 29th

I made it through the week without seeing Lorenzo again. Okay, maybe I did everything I possibly could to *avoid* seeing him. I came in early, ate lunch at my desk, and practically ran out of the building at 5 pm. One of my favorite parts of the office is that it's a ten minute walk from my apartment. The gym I do my pilates classes at is in between the two, so I stop there on my walk home.

It's 4:30 pm on Friday, and the employees are buzzing with the excitement of the long weekend for New Year's. I can't help but feel excited, too. I'm the only one still working as everyone else waits out the clock. Victor is telling me about the trip he and his boyfriend are taking for the weekend while I finish organizing the files for the audit.

At 4:50, we start cleaning our desks and packing our bags. A ding sounds from my computer and I groan. Who the hell would be writing to me just before the holiday weekend? I unlock my computer and open Teams, the messaging app our company uses.

Lorenzo Mancini: what are your plans this weekend

My stomach drops and fills with butterflies. I've done my best this week to put the Lorenzo mistake box on the same 'did not happen' shelf as the Trent run-in box. I knew it was a matter of time before

I'd run into him again, but I figured by then I'd be over the whole situation. And by whole situation, I mean him.

I couldn't stop thinking about his kisses and the way his hands felt on my body. I couldn't stop wishing for that cord to be around my neck again, completely at his mercy. Something about Lorenzo felt so intoxicating, but I knew it was just a facade. It was part of his charm, and it was not reserved for me.

He made that clear, and I accepted it. I have no business falling for a guy like him. So I refuse to do it.

But his message makes it very clear that try as I might, I can't help the effect he has on me. A part of me, the logical one, wants to ignore his message. In nine minutes, I can log off and ignore this over the long weekend.

But the other part of me, the louder, stupider, hopeless romantic one, wants me to answer.

> Kate Appleton: Just the usual. Hang out with my best friend, pilates, Felix and Friends.

I hover over the send button, wondering if my response is appropriate. Why exactly is he writing to me? And after all this time, too?

I hit enter before I can lose my nerve. When he doesn't start typing after a minute, I send another message.

> Me: Maybe I'll venture out and start a new series with the extra days off.

After two minutes, I lock my screen again. I'm not going to hang around waiting for his response. Plus, we've got 6 minutes before it's time to go. I finish packing my bag, undocking my laptop to take it home just in case. Maybe I'll do some extra work and get ahead if I'm bored.

At 4:59, I hear the ping from my bag. I dive into it and open my laptop, keying in the password before I can think it through.

Lorenzo Mancini: come to my friends new years party

What in the world? I probably should have seen an invitation coming, but it seems so oppositional to the no boyfriend, fun-for-a-night stance he took. Why would he be inviting me to *his* friend's party when he hasn't even tried to see or talk to me again?

For heaven's sake, he hasn't even asked for my number.

Then he does that thing again, where it's like he's reading my mind. He sends a message with his phone number. I store it into my cell and pocket it, then tuck my laptop back into my bag.

I'll ruminate over this and decide if it's a good idea or not.

• • • ● • ● • • •

I've ruminated, and I know it's a bad idea. But screw it to all hell, I texted him. Just one word: Kate. I toss my bag on my bed and change out of my exercise clothes, heading to the shower.

I'm leaving the ball in his court. He needs to explain himself if this is going to be a thing. Maybe he wants to be friends with benefits.

But does he have others? That's something I should ask him, right? For safety purposes.

That's what I keep telling myself, at least. The true reason, which I hate to admit, is that I feel that burn of jealousy in my throat when I think about how many women he's slept with. How he went back to Rowan's party and *took shots* off someone else.

Can I make peace with just being a fun fling for this guy? What if he just wants to be friends?

Yeah, right. A guy doesn't sleep with you and then invite you to a party out of friendship. Did he invite Sara, too? Did he leave with her from the party? Or worse, take her upstairs?

Dread fills me at the thought of him doing what he did with me on the same bed. With the same Christmas lights.

I have so many questions, and I'm dying for answers. When I finish drying off, I lay in bed and pull up my messages, typing Victor's name. Then I rethink before typing out a message. If I ask him if Lorenzo left with her, it's a dead giveaway as to why. We don't work in the same department, and I don't know him outside of this job. Or the holiday party, really.

Instead, I start searching for him on social media, now that I have his last name. After various searches, even through the web, I'm unable to locate a profile.

Weird.

I really want to know what he's playing at and who he is. Going to this New Year's party would at least get me answers. Yes. I'll go to this party, demand he explain himself.

I'm not sure if I can make peace with knowing he's just a fling. But I *do* know I can't make peace with not finding out.

• • • • • • • • • •

"He texted you?" Char exclaims, tucking her legs underneath her on my bed. She's dressed in tight leggings and a super cute, knit sweater, her makeup completely done. She's going out with someone later tonight.

"He wrote to me on Teams first, then he gave me his number. I just explained all of this to you."

"Yeah, yeah, semantics. But he hasn't answered your text?"

"Nope." I glance down to hide my worry, but Char knows me better than anyone.

"What kind of date starts at 10 pm?" I question in an attempt to distract her.

She wiggles her eyebrows at me and says, "The fun kind."

I chuckle and lean back on my pillows.

"He's probably busy." Oh, Char and her optimism. "He'll text you back, I know it."

"You can't know that. You don't know him."

"Why would he give you his number if he didn't want to talk to you?" she counters.

As I open my mouth to retort that he's an enigma that makes no sense to me, so who knows why, my phone buzzes. My eyes widen and Char starts clapping.

I shoot up and reach for my phone on the nightstand. "Let's see who it is before—"

Lorenzo message

"Ugh, he would have an Android," I say, pretending I'm not doing an internal happy dance at the sight of his name on my screen.

"Open it, open it!" Char squeals.

Lorenzo: so you did text me

What in the world am I supposed to do with that?

"Oh my god, he for sure likes you," Char says in my ear, having read the message over my shoulder. I nudge her away and type out my response.

> Me: Obviously, that's why you got an incoming message

"Let me see!" Char snatches the phone out of my hand before I can stop her and reads my reply. "Jeez, Kate, why do you have to be so dry?"

"What? It's true. He got my message, why does he have to point it out?"

"Maybe he thought you wouldn't text him. You didn't even reply to his message on Times or whatever that work app is called."

"Teams," I correct. Char owns her own small company for interior design and has never worked a desk job a day in her life. But damn, she does have a point about Lorenzo. "Ugh, I suck at this shit!" I grab my phone from her, prepared to toss it, when the vibration of an incoming message stops me.

> Lorenzo: does this mean youre giving in

His lack of punctuation annoys me. And giving in to what? Char's at my shoulder again and she gasps.

"What? What?" I ask when she doesn't explain.

"He has to be referencing your dark side."

"I don't *have* a dark side."

Char quirks a brow and leans back on her hands. "Oh, really? So you *didn't* assault your ex-boyfriend and—"

"Okay, okay! God, you're worse than he is. You're supposed to be on my side."

"I *am* on your side, Kate. But you're in denial. What's wrong with having some fun with Lorenzo? So what if it can't go anywhere?"

I gape at her. "It's just, it's not who I am! I don't even want a boyfriend right now—"

"Exactly! That's why this is perfect. Have some fun with the guy, and when you're bored or ready to settle down, dump his ass and move on. Obviously, he can handle it. He told you himself he's not looking to be your boyfriend."

"He took shots off Sara!"

"And? That doesn't mean anything. It also means *you* can do whatever you want. You're not tied down."

She's making a lot of sense, but my heart still beats its warning. "What if I get hurt?"

"You can't be hurt if you only do what you want. You have the power here, Kate. Own it."

I reread Lorenzo's message while I process what Char said.

"That's why they say 'careful what you wish for'. Your genie just acted really fast." I chuckle, partially at her humor and partially out of nerves. "Text him back!"

She moves over my shoulder and I reluctantly start to type out a message.

Me: Giving in to what?

Char stops me before I hit send. "No, no, no! Turn your flirt on."

"Fine, what would you have me say?"

"Here." She takes the phone from my hand and starts typing rapidly.

"Show me before you send anything!"

"Sorry, already sent." I dive at her.

"Ahhhh! Why did you do that?" I grab my phone from her and fix myself as she laughs.

"It's nothing crazy, just read it."

> Me: depends what you're referring to ;)

If I could melt into the mattress and disappear from the mortification, I would. Before I can bitch Char out, Lorenzo's reply comes through.

> Lorenzo: you giving into your true desires is what im referring to

"Who is he to tell me what my true desires are?" I shout indignantly. Char starts to laugh but covers it with a cough when I pierce her with a murderous glare.

"Look. Do you want to see him again, or not?" Char asks me in all seriousness.

"Yeah, I do," I respond automatically. Then I quickly add, "I need answers."

She gives me a disbelieving look. "Then see him. See where it takes you." Something about her words hits home, and I nod slowly.

"Yeah. Yeah, okay, I think I will."

> Me: Where is this New Year's party at?

He replies with two messages: one with the address and one with the time.

> Me: This is on 12/31, right?

> Lorenzo: yes princess the night everyone celebrates

I don't appreciate his tone. There's nothing wrong with making sure of the date.

> Me: Okay. I'll let you know if I'll be attending.

"Kate! Why do you have to sound like this is a business meeting and not a hot date?" Before I can respond, she continues, "And what do you mean, you'll let him know? You just said you want to go!"

"I thought playing hard to get was a thing! Isn't that what I'm supposed to be doing?"

Char laughs, then glances down at my phone when the screen lights up with his response.

> Lorenzo: see you there

Chapter Nine

December 31st

This was a mistake. Trying to be bold, I didn't text him back. He was so sure I would come, so I decided I didn't need to confirm. And *maybe* a small part of me hoped that he would follow up. But it's 8 o'clock sharp and the Uber just dropped me off in front of the house he sent the address to. I see his car parked in the driveway, as shiny as it was six days ago, and I'm filled with nerves.

I pull down the short hem of my very tight, long-sleeved black dress. It's somewhat pointless, because I have black, fleece-lined tights underneath, but I'm uncomfortable. Char insisted on taking me shopping after brunch and she made me try on way too many dresses. It was hard to even tell them apart, they were so similar—black, short, and revealing. This one felt the longest to me, landing at mid-thigh with a shallow v-cut.

I hold the gold and black intertwined strap of my otherwise black purse and walk up in my black heels. My hair is in its usual bun, and I added a curl on each side of my face like I did for the holiday party.

Because Lorenzo liked playing with them, and I thought he might like them again tonight. Pathetic, I know. At least I didn't wear my glasses, too. I have *some* self-restraint.

I walk up the long, pebbled path to the cozy house. It's made of brick with a gray shingle roof, and the front door is painted a matching maroon.

I take a deep breath, boosting my confidence by reminding myself I'm getting answers tonight. I knock on the door and take a step back. A few long, nerve-wracking moments later, a large, tall man opens the door. He reminds me of Lorenzo in the way he's dressed, with all black clothes and a ring through his lip. He sizes me up before looking me dead in the eye.

"Who are you?"

"H-Hi, I'm Kate," I stammer. When he cocks an eyebrow, I add hesitantly, "Lorenzo invited me?"

"Yo! Zo! There's someone here for you!" the man shouts into the house. He stays at the entrance, though, hovering over the door and staring at me. I shuffle uncomfortably but luckily, Lorenzo walks up a few seconds later.

"Kate," he says. His voice has that same silk I thought I previously imagined, and his eyes rake over my body. I watch them fill with smoke and my stomach swoops under his very lustful perusal.

"Hey," I say, trying to play it cool. I'm happy to hear that I sound totally normal and not afraid and excited and unsure, like I actually feel. I clutch my purse but don't move, the other guy still standing in the doorway causing me pause.

"Move, Santi," Lorenzo says, pushing past who I can only assume is his friend. Santi releases the door and retreats into the house. Lorenzo shuts the door behind him and stands in front of me.

"You look stunning," he says, pure sex dripping from his lips.

"Oh, thanks. Um, you, too," I reply awkwardly, taking in his appearance. He has on a similar outfit to what he wore the first night I met him—black jeans, black boots, and a long-sleeved black shirt.

"You came alone?" he questions, glancing behind me.

"Yeah. I wasn't aware I could invite anyone..."

He chuckles, and I see that familiar twinkle in his eye. I hate how seeing it makes me feel like I'm floating on a cloud. "It's a party, of course you can bring someone."

He could have told me that. Char would have loved to come. "Well, it's just me. Hope that's okay."

"It's more than okay. It's great."

I nod, and we stand for a moment, holding each other captive with our eyes. I get that same feeling that he's completely fine just watching me. I, on the other hand, want to squirm under his watch and run the six miles back home.

"Should we...?" I point towards the door, but Lorenzo doesn't break eye contact.

"Yeah, let's go." He doesn't move, so I take it upon myself to walk past him. When I turn back to make sure he's following, because I'm not going to walk into his friend's house without him, his eyes are traveling my body.

I turn back to the door and open it, a small smile playing on my lips. I love the effect I seem to have on him, even if it is just on a physical level. The memory of him slapping my butt flashes across my mind and I bite down on my lower lip.

"You're early, but people will start showing up soon," he says, sidling up next to me. We walk across the living room and through a door, propped open by a jamb, that leads to the patio.

"Didn't you say 8?"

"Yeah, but no one's ever actually on time." He grins at me and guides me to some patio chairs facing the pool. I bite my tongue rather than start a lecture about the importance of punctuality. Char insisted, more than once, that I needed to tone down my "Kateisms," as she calls them.

There's a beer pong table set up in the lawn across from the pool, where two guys have a game going. Aren't we a little old to be playing these college games? Then again, it is New Year's. And Lorenzo doesn't strike me as the type of person to care what one "should" be doing.

He plops down on one of the patio couches and I hesitate, unsure if I should sit next to him or in one of the individual chairs. Lorenzo decides for me, chuckling and pulling on my arm so I drop next to him.

The feel of his fingers on my skin is all consuming, and it makes me realize that it's the first time he's touched me since arriving. He didn't hug me or kiss me... not even a damn handshake.

But I guess that's normal for a guy I barely know who I've hooked up with once. It would be foolish of me to expect a kiss at midnight. The nerves start to take over again, and I wonder if I really did make a mistake in coming here tonight.

"Want something to drink?" Lorenzo asks, his eyes roaming over the few people spread along the patio. Besides the beer pong guys, the man who opened the door is speaking with a DJ, and a couple of girls are near a table with drinks. There doesn't seem to be any food at this party.

"Yeah, sure," I reply, regretting not having eaten dinner. But what kind of party doesn't have food?

Lorenzo stands up and heads towards the drink table, leaving me alone. I rub my thumb against the nail on my index finger, a nervous habit I've had ever since I can remember. It feels less obvious than nail biting, and for some reason it soothes me. It's as if I can rub out the nervous energy with the feel of my nail digging into my skin.

Lorenzo returns quickly carrying two black cups; the only festive items here, it seems. *This is the perfect time for my questions.*

"To the new year," he says, handing me a cup. As we raise them, he adds, "And to badassery."

This time, I don't roll my eyes. I laugh.

• • • • ● • ● • • •

"Wooo!" My exclamation of joy after sinking the ball into the cup sounds foreign to me. I've had at least four drinks, but I can't be positive because I have no idea how much is actually in these cups.

Turns out, they weren't playing beer pong. It's shot pong. The shots are Fireball, which I'm enjoying tonight more than ever before because the cinnamon reminds me of Lorenzo.

Where is he, anyway? My fuzzy brain tries to remember where he last went, but then my pong partner, Larissa, bumps her shoulder into mine.

"Kate, you're awesome!" she slurs. She's a lot more drunk than she was when she asked me to play with her.

Oh, that's right! Lorenzo kept getting up to say hi to all his friends who arrived. I'd wait on the patio couch as he gave them one of those guy handshakes, where they slap hands and slide their fingers through. I've secretly always wanted to do that with someone.

Each time I'd summon the courage to ask about Sara, or what any of this means, or why he's not on social media, he'd up and leave again.

Sometimes they'd disappear into the house, other times he'd return right back to his seat next to me. He refilled our cups twice with a drink he called a French 57. Or maybe it was 75. I shrug and then laugh when I realize I'm shrugging to my own thoughts.

When Lorenzo went into the house with a group of guys and the alcohol infiltrated my system, I walked over to the drink table to refill my cup. It was really serving its purpose, easing me and stopping the hamster wheel from turning. That's when Larissa, flanked by two other girls, came over and asked if I wanted to play a round of shot pong with them.

I felt brave enough with the drinks in me to say yes, even if they were a hell of a lot prettier than me. I was able to ignore the light intimidation I felt by being here, because the only person I know kept disappearing on me.

I should be more upset about it. I was before. But after two rounds of shot pong, nothing really seems to matter anymore.

"Who did you say you're here with again?" One of Larissa's friends asks. I can't remember their names to save my life.

"I invited her." His voice sets all the hairs on my body standing up, despite the numbness I feel inside. I smile involuntarily and turn around, finding Lorenzo taking the last step towards me.

"There you are," I say loudly, my own words coming out a bit slurred. I hold my hand out for one of those guy handshakes, but he just raises his eyebrows in amusement.

"Are you drunk?"

"You know, I think I am," I say with a giggle.

"We really like her, Zo," Larissa says, coming to stand beside me and slinging her arm around my shoulder. I catch her friends on the other side of the pong table, and it doesn't seem like they share the sentiment.

Fuck them.

"How old are you?" I blurt out. Half of Lorenzo's lips tilt up, revealing his dimple.

"Twenty-three."

"I'm twenty-five." My nose wrinkles.

Lorenzo shrugs. "Just a number."

"I'm twenty-three, too," Larissa interjects. I turn my head to the side to look at her and find myself appreciating how nice and welcoming she's been. If it wasn't for her, I know I wouldn't be having a good time. Impulsively, and alcohol driven, I land a kiss right on her cheek. She giggles but then I'm yanked away by a calloused and strong hand gripping my arm.

"Ow!"

"Oh, stop, I know you've felt worse," Lorenzo purrs. I'm standing next to him now, though I'm not exactly sure how that happened. His words process slowly, but when they do, I search around me to see if anyone heard him.

"Chill, princess. No one here works with us."

I guess that's true. I'm trying to muster up the annoyance I should feel at the fact that he's not understanding—or ignoring—the *no one* part, but it's hidden beneath the fog and I don't care enough to find it. His touch feels good, and standing next to him does funny things to me.

"Play shot pong with us," I tell him.

"How many rounds have you guys played?" He eyes the table that I didn't realize was littered with empty cups from the third round we were playing. There are some spills, too. When did that happen?

"This was our fourth game," Larissa says.

"No, thiiiird," I say, drawing out the last word. I sound ridiculous, and I don't care. It's great. I start to giggle. "I'm never too drunk for numbers!"

"Come on, let's get you some water," Lorenzo says. He takes my hand and tows me across the yard and into the house.

"Am I allowed to be in here?" I ask. I trip over the door jamb, but Lorenzo is there instantly, steadying me with his arms. He laughs and shakes his head, guiding me into the small kitchen on the immediate right.

When I'm in front of the counter, I lean on it and stare at him with a goofy grin. He puts his hands on my waist and hoists me onto the counter, then grabs a cup from the stack of the same black cups next to the fridge.

"How many drinks have you had?" he asks as he fills the cup from the dispenser on the door.

"I'm allowed to drink as much or as little as I please," I say defiantly. Although I'm not making a good case for myself by swaying a bit.

"Of course you are, princess. I'm just trying to assess the situation, see what I'm working with here."

"I like when you call me princess," I say thoughtlessly. I throw my hand over my mouth once the words register in the space between us. He hands me the cup of water and steps in between my thighs, placing his hands on my knees.

"But you were so insistent I not call you that."

I take a sip of water. "Yeah, around our employees. I mean Rowan's employees. Our coworkers. At—"

"I got it, Kate." He laughs and I join him, feeling much more at ease than when I'd first arrived.

"I've had like five drinks or something. The three you gave me, and then whatever I drank in the shot pong. Oh, but I refilled one..."

I think back, trying to calculate, but his scrutinizing look causes me to ask, "What?"

"I feel like you shouldn't be that drunk..."

I ponder his words. I drank about as much when we were at Rowan's party. I drink at brunches with Char, and sometimes I'll have wine at home, so it's not like I don't have a tolerance.

"I didn't eat!" I shout when I remember.

"Ah. That'll do it."

"Actually, I am kinda—"

"Zo! You in for a game of pong?" The guy that answered the door when I arrived is standing at the patio door, looking directly at Lorenzo, as if I'm not even here. Lorenzo slides his hands off my knees, taking a small step back.

"Nah, maybe later." The guy gives me a brief glance before returning outside. I hear the music lightly from here, but I'm grateful they're not blasting it.

"Why do they all call you Zo?"

He shrugs. "That's what my friends call me."

Friends. "Oh." I guess I'm not his friend, then. I don't know what I am.

Lorenzo lifts my chin with a finger. "You can call me Zo if you want."

I beam at him, drunk enough that I don't care to express my feelings. "Come on, let's go play pong! I was doing so well."

"Drink more water first." I don't like that he's making demands of me, but I figure it's probably a good idea. "And if I have to step away, don't go wandering. Stay with Larissa or Maria."

"Who's Maria?"

"She was playing pong against you and Larissa." *So that's her name.*

"I don't think she liked me," I confess.

"She doesn't like most people. Don't worry about it."

There's something in his voice that makes me want to question him, but I refrain.

Chapter Ten

December 31st

Larissa and I lost both rounds of shot pong to Lorenzo and Santi, the guy who opened the door for me when I first arrived. Turns out, he's the host of this party. Despite our losses, Larissa and I would hug and high five each time we made a shot. She was just as friendly as earlier, and I find that I'd really like to get to know her. Santi remained standoffish, particularly when Lorenzo would wink at me from across the table.

It didn't bother me the way it should, though. Between the level of drunkenness I've now reached and the giddiness from Lorenzo's flirting, I couldn't be bothered by his strange behavior. When Lorenzo landed the ball in the last cup, I held his gaze as I took the shot, the cinnamon whiskey burning down my throat and making me want *his* cinnamon taste instead.

Lorenzo walks up to me as Larissa pretends to cry over losing. He wraps his arms around my waist, pulling me into him. I inhale deeply and sigh. I'm not sure if it's because I already have cinnamon on my breath, but he smells more like smoke now. He brings his lips to my ear and whispers, "Come with me."

He links his hand with mine, this time interlaced, and pulls me into the house. The need for secrecy drowned in the Fireball. He leads me past the kitchen and down a hallway, opening the first door on the right. As soon as he closes the door, I stumble into him, crashing my lips onto his.

He meets me with equal fervor, our tongues clashing and swirling against each other. I moan and a rumble erupts from his chest. I don't have it in me to pretend that I don't want this, because I don't think I've ever wanted something so badly.

"Even greedier than last time, I see," he murmurs against my lips. I grin in response, feeling so light and carefree. I just want to get lost in him.

"Do what you promised. Ruin me," I say between heated kisses.

"First time wasn't enough for you?"

"I want more."

We keep our lips moving between our words. He guides us to the bed and pulls me onto him seamlessly, our mouths never parting.

"Why can't we do this at one of our places?"

"That feels too..." he breaks off the kiss and stares into my eyes, brushing a curl back. "Intimate."

I laugh. "You make no sense to me."

"I've been told that once or twice." He brings his lips to mine but I pull back, placing my hands on his chest to peer down at him.

"Are you just sleeping with a bunch of people?" I came here for answers, and I need to get them.

"Not currently. Only you," he says, his eyes open and studying me.

"Oh." That's not the answer I expected.

"Is this going to be a problem for you?"

"What?"

"This. Doing what we're doing."

"What exactly is it that we're doing?"

"Having fun. I thought I made that clear."

"You did. I'm having trouble understanding exactly what that means, though."

He laughs. "Of course you are. It means whatever we want it to mean. If you need a label, I guess friends with benefits works. If you want to be more vague about it, we're two people who happen to work at the same place that enjoy fucking each other from time to time."

I don't like his insinuation that I need a label, even if it's true. But my body pressed on his paired with his kissable lips make it so I don't care. I want him to consume me, right now. I don't need to ruin it with my annoying questions.

"So, is that going to be a problem?" He implores me with his penetrating stare.

"Kiss me," I say breathlessly. He wastes no time in giving me what I want. He takes my head in his and brings my face closer to his. He tastes just as he did last time. I had convinced myself that I wouldn't ever get to have him again, so I lose myself.

His pelvis thrusts into mine, my dress sliding up my thighs and his jeans pushing into my core. My clit throbs in response, and I want to tear our clothes off.

I clutch at the shirt on his chest, realizing it's not a button down like last time. I pull at the bottom and lift it up, our lips only parting when the shirt passes over his head. I rub my hands over his shoulders and chest as he massages my breasts, our tongues moving steadily against each other. My nipples harden against my black lace bra, and I grow impatient as he simply rubs against them.

I tug at the bottom of my dress but his hands swiftly grab my wrists. He takes them both in one hand, then slides his free hand under my dress and caresses my pussy. I moan and pulse my hips into him, refusing to break our kiss to tell him to take me now.

I can feel his rock hard dick pressing into his jeans, which in turn is pressing onto my opening. If we weren't wearing clothes, he'd slip right in.

"Fuck, you feel so good, Kate," he says against my lips, then sucks my bottom lip into his mouth. I nibble at his upper lip, and he smirks. "Don't be scared. I like it rough."

Okay. I bite down a bit harder, and a growl erupts from his throat. My pussy tightens in response. If I wasn't in a steady haze of alcohol and lust, I'd probably wonder why I'm so turned on by this. But I don't question it, simply giving in to the pleasure.

Without warning, I'm flipped onto my back and he's hovering over me, his knee between my thighs and his hooded gaze all over me. He grips my dress and pulls it off so quickly, my body bounces into the mattress.

I meet his eyes and all I can see is desire. *For me.* It stirs something deep inside me, and my lips part in awe. He slides his hands from my hips to my bra, taking my full breasts into his hands and squeezing gently.

"I want to keep you coming back for more, princess. You're mine for as long as I see fit."

In the real world, his words would have me running for the hills. Right now, I nod my head eagerly and spread my legs a little wider. He pulls one of my breasts out and trails kisses down my neck, collarbone, and chest, finally settling on my exposed nipple.

His tongue swirls around it, causing my back to arch. He sucks it into his mouth while tilting his head up to look at me. When my eyes meet his, he bites my nipple so hard I scream. His hand flies up to cover my mouth and my eyes widen until they burn.

His eyes are boring into mine, not a hint of mercy present. He licks the soft skin around my nipple, which throbs in pain until his tongue soothes it. He uses the tip to circle around the exact place where it stings, and it's so soothing that my eyes roll into the back of my head.

"You're doing so good, baby. I know you're going to take me so well." He sucks my nipple into his mouth then releases it with a pop, replacing the bra over it. The lace rubs on the sore spots where I'm convinced there are indentations from his teeth.

He kisses across to the other breast, but he doesn't free it. He sucks the exposed skin and his hand returns to stroking my pussy through my panties. I'm so wet that his fingers slide in through the fabric.

I buck my hips into him and move my hand to the buttons of his jeans, but again he stops me by grabbing my wrist and tucking my hand under my butt. He tortures me further by shifting his body up so his jeans covered dick is right over my pussy, and he presses into me.

I moan and thread my fingers through his hair. "Stop teasing me."

He looks up at me, a glint in his eye. "I'll do whatever I want."

I'm not sure what makes me do it—unfiltered desire, the look in his eye, or knowing he gets off on the control. "Please," I whisper, my bottom lip jutting out in a pout.

His eyebrows raise by a fraction, and if I didn't know better, I'd think I actually surprised him. "Such a good girl."

He climbs off the bed and holds me in his gaze as he pops the button on his jeans, then slowly pulls down the zipper. His black boxer briefs are low on his hips, and he pulls them off with his also black jeans. I watch his cock spring free, standing erect in the air.

I don't have the confidence he has, not even close. My eyes roam over his torso, then land on his face. His hooded gaze is on me, waiting to pounce like I'm his prey. I bite down on my lip and he opens the side table drawer, pulling out a condom.

Did he put that there?

He drops the foil next to my leg on the bed and pulls my matching lace panties off, letting them drop to the floor. I start to scoot up on the bed but he grabs my knees, yanking me closer to him.

"When are you going to learn some patience, princess? Huh?" His eyes move to my pussy as he slides his index finger up my slit. "When are you going to learn that you have no control here?"

My eyes widen as he paints my inner thigh with the wetness from that one finger. He lowers to his knees in front of me and runs the tip of his tongue over his lower lip before bringing his mouth to my clit and sucking.

My free hand grips the bed sheet while the one stuck under my butt digs into the cheek. He uses the tip of his tongue to lick my clit far too lightly. I moan, lifting my hips to meet his tongue. He moves one hand to my hip, holding me down. The other hand comes to the entrance of my pussy, but he only puts the pad of a finger inside.

My walls clench, trying to suck him in so I can feel more. He alternates between sucks and licks of my clit, driving me crazy. Just as the feeling heightens from one, he switches and it comes back down. It's like an orgasmic wave, and I'm being ripped through its current.

He swirls the bit of finger he has in me, then moves his finger past the skin below my pussy and over my asshole.

On reflex, I use my hands to pull me back. His tongue stops touching my clit and he looks up at me.

I wait for him to speak, but he doesn't. A few beats pass, and he slides the hand on my hip to the back of my knee, pulling me towards him. He looks at me one last time, but when I don't say anything, he brings his mouth back to my clit and pushes the pad of his finger, dripping with my desire, into my tight hole.

It slides right in, and I clench around it. The effect is instantaneous—the sucking of my clit feels like fireworks exploding, shooting to the ends of me. I'm moaning non-stop, but I can hardly hear myself through the all-consuming high that's taken over. He presses the finger in me down, and I feel a pressure as he switches to licking my clit.

I explode, mind, body, and spirit. My grip on my ass becomes bruising. My head tilts back as I call out his name. When the orgasm subsides, he removes his finger and moves his mouth to my thigh, licking the soft skin.

Then, he bites it. Harder than he bit my nipple.

"Fuck!" I shout, my senses being forced back to earth.

"I need you alert, baby girl. Had to make sure I didn't put you in a coma there." I glare at him, angry that he's stealing my pleasure. But all I get in return is that stupid smirk.

He stands up, licks his lips, and grabs the condom next to me. He tears it open with his teeth, tossing the packaging, then rolls the latex onto his dick. He grabs my knees, his touch weakening me, and pulls me to the edge of the bed.

"You ready?" He looks directly into my eye. I give him a quizzical look but nod, unsure why he needs me to confirm.

When he thrusts into me, I realize why. I'm not sure how I thought he was going hard and fast last time. He doesn't give me a moment to adjust or catch my breath. He thrusts in and out of me at high speed, my thighs tightening of their own accord.

He places his hands on them and pushes them open, then lifts my legs and places my knees over his elbows. His dick hits me so deep, repeatedly, and his pelvis hits my too-sensitive clit. It's too much, way too much, and my body keeps trying to close him out.

"You can handle it, baby." I focus on keeping my legs limp. "That's it, princess. You're doing so good. Look how you're taking me."

I follow his gaze to the place where our bodies keep connecting, and I try to stop myself from panting and whimpering. But before long, the whimpers turn into moans and the pants turn into gasps of pleasure. The sensitivity on my clit has quickly evolved to orgasmic need, pulsing with each tap of his pelvis as he moves in and out.

"You don't need to be silent here, there's no one that cares to know." His words remind me of us at Rowan's and it escalates my pleasure. I remember the lights around my neck and I wish we had them now.

Feeling brave, I decide to share my thoughts. "Too bad we don't have those Christmas lights."

He leans in and his devilish grin comes slow. "I do have these." He shakes his hands at me before striking at my throat, his grip bruising in the best way possible. I moan as he continues his relentless pounding, which now feels exactly right rather than too much.

"Come for me again, princess. I want to hear my name on those luscious lips," Lorenzo says, sweat beading on his body from his exertion. Cinnamon and smoke is all I can smell, and I collapse my head back on the bed as the climax nears. He applies pressure to my throat, constricting my air flow, and my eyes roll into my head. My orgasm rolls over me, not as suddenly as last time, but with equal intensity.

"Say my name, baby," Lorenzo begs, his thrusts increasing even more.

It takes me a moment through my orgasm to hear him, but I give him what he wants. "Oh, Lorenzo," I rasp, despite my constricted airway.

Then he groans my name as he follows me, and I can see why he liked hearing it. His dick is all the way deep, and he lands on top of me, breathing heavily with his eyes closed.

After a few moments, he wraps his arms around my waist and turns us onto his back. I collapse on top of him, high on alcohol, my orgasms, and him. Our chests rise and fall in synchronicity. I lay my head on his shoulder and close my eyes, reveling in the feeling of us. I'm so sated and completely limp, I just want to sleep.

I squint my eyes to peek at him, and I find him watching me. His eyes are hooded, but not the way they were before. For all the amused looks and smirks he usually wears, I didn't expect his expression of joy to look like he does now. His eyes are lighter, and his lips are tilted up with his dimples on display.

He doesn't say anything, and I don't either. I don't want to ruin this moment by speaking, or remembering that it's just for tonight. I adjust my head to his chest and close my eyes, snuggling in while I can. As I'm about to fall asleep, Lorenzo slides me off of him. When he rises from the bed, I lift my head.

"Sorry, I didn't mean to wake you."

"Where are you going?" I don't recognize my voice, whispered and loose.

"I'm going back out. You can sleep here though, I'll tell Santi."

"No, no. I'll get up."

"Do you want me to order you an Uber?"

What in the world? He's kicking me out?

His hot and cold act is getting to me and I hold back the tears that are threatening to spill over. "Uh, no, I can do it. I need my phone though." Lorenzo pulls his boxers and jeans on at once, zipping and buttoning them before digging in my purse.

"Here." The screen lights up and we both glance down at it.

Notification at 11:59: Brad on Tinder

Bonus Chapter

Want to read December 22nd in Lorenzo's POV?
Use this QR code:

Also By Amanda Bentley

Drift

The Holiday Hookup (Festive Fun # 1)
Struck by Stupid (Festive Fun # 2)
Sh*t Out of Luck (Festive Fun # 3)

Acknowledgments

To my alpha readers: Madeleine, Arley, and Sabrina. You have no idea how much your thoughts help me. It gets lonely in my writer world when I have ideas that need sharing, and you guys are just the cure. Thank you for supporting me in your own ways!

To all my beta readers: Ava, Cassie, Emily, Kaitlyn, Kath, Jordan V, and Jordy. Thank you for providing the necessary feedback to help shape the story! And, of course, for your support.

To A.R. Rose: thank you for being a sincerely giving friend. I'm obsessed with this cover. You saved the world from Grandma scrawl!

And finally, as always, thanks to YOU: the reader!

Amanda Bentley loves escaping into fictional worlds through reading and writing. A typical Pisces, she's as much a mood writer as she is a mood reader. She likes her book boyfriends morally grey, but she'll read any book with romance (preferably drenched in spice and angst).

When she's not writing, you might find her chasing her wild toddler, or on stage, performing improv with her husband. She's a creative, free spirit, and while she loves a fun adventure, there's no place like her bed with a book.

Amanda can be found on TikTok and Instagram under @amandabentleybooks. Her DM's are always open!

Made in the USA
Columbia, SC
13 February 2023